The Immigrs

FROM SWITZERLAND TO AMERICA

THE JOURNEY OF
Elisa

NANCY PARKER BRUMMETT

Cook

Be sure to read all the books in
The Immigrants' Chronicles

The Journey of Emilie
The Journey of Hannah
The Journey of Pieter and Anna
The Journey of Elisa
The Journey of Yung Lee

Cook Communications Ministries,
Colorado Springs, Colorado 80918
Cook Communications, Paris, Ontario
Kingsway Communications, Eastbourne, England

THE JOURNEY OF ELISA
© 2000 by Nancy Parker Brummett

Edited by Kathy Davis
Design by PAZ Design Group and Dana Sherrer of iDesignEtc.
Art direction by Kelly S. Robinson
Cover illustration by Cheri Bladholm

First printing, 2000
Printed in the United States of America
04 03 02 01 00   5 4 3 2 1

Library of Congress Cataloging-in-Publication Data

Brummett, Nancy Parker.
   The journey of Elisa : from Switzerland to America /
   Nancy Parker Brummett.
        p. cm. — (The immigrants chronicles)
   Summary: When her father's illness causes the family to move from
Brazil to Tennessee to be near their Swiss relatives, eleven-year-old Elisa
finds that her family's faith sustains them through a number of trials.
   ISBN 0-7814-3286-3
   [1. Swiss Americans—Fiction. 2. Family life—Tennessee—Fiction.
3. Christian life—Fiction. 4. Tennessee—Fiction.] I. Title. II. Series.

PZ7+
[Fic]—dc21   99-041981

Acknowledgments

I am indebted to my great-grandmother, Elisa Bolli Buffat, and my great-grandfather, Alfred Buffat, for writing the memoirs that gave me insight into the lives they lived. I am also indebted to David Babelay, himself a descendent of the French-Swiss in East Tennessee, for compiling all the memoirs, diaries, and letters of this brave colony of immigrants into two volumes titled, *They Trusted and Were Delivered: The French-Swiss of Knoxville, Tennessee*. A special thank you to David and to Alyson Shaffer, 12, for reading this manuscript and giving me their thoughts. Most of all I am grateful for my father, John Alfred Parker, who instilled in me respect and curiosity for all those who came before.

Dedication

For Francesca, Amanda, and Eleanor—through you, the story continues.

Chapter One

Elisa Bolli kicked her feet softly against the bottom rail of the big wooden chair in her father's office. As she had on countless Saturday mornings, she was waiting for him to finish his work so the two of them could shop in the marketplace.

"Not too much longer, *ma chérie*," her father said as he entered figures into a large, leather-bound ledger.

Elisa knew her father, Edouard Bolli, was an important man in Pernambuco, the coastal port in Brazil where her family had lived since he was appointed Swiss Consul. But she wasn't thinking about his duties as Consul or the record keeping that he had to do for his dry goods business that morning. She just wanted him to finish his work.

While she waited, Elisa picked through a bowl of nuts on the table beside her, choosing the sweet cashews and leaving the big Brazil nuts behind.

Every fifth Saturday it was Elisa's turn to accompany her father into town while her three sisters and brother stayed at home. Although Elisa had enjoyed many such Saturday mornings before, this one was special.

Elisa was almost eleven years old, and her father had promised her a special birthday gift from one of the shops in town. It was also special because Elisa knew it was the last time she would sit in this richly paneled office and look out at the ships in the harbor below as she waited for her father. Before it was her turn to have another Saturday morning with him, her family would sail for North America to join her mother's Swiss relatives in East Tennessee.

"What will become of this furniture when we go, Papa?" Elisa asked as she looked around the room at the big Brazilwood desk and credenza. "Will we be taking it with us?"

"No, dear, it belongs to the consulate. Now be still just a bit longer. No more questions, please. The fewer distractions I have, the sooner we can go shopping."

Elisa couldn't imagine her father not sitting behind the big desk with the marble top. She remembered the day her sister Cecile had agreed to share her Saturday morning with Elisa and the two of them had played house under the desk with their dolls. She wondered who would be sitting in the big leather chair after her father left, but she didn't dare interrupt him to ask. Instead, she just crunched on a mouthful of cashew nuts and listened to the tick-tock-tick of the mantel clock and the scritch-scratch-scritch of her father's pen on paper.

Elisa was too hot to move. Because this was a special Saturday morning with Papa, Mama had agreed to let her wear the white cotton dress with the high lace collar usually kept freshly bleached for Sundays. Josepha, the black cook, had braided Elisa's dark hair on the sides and fastened the two braids in back with a large white bow. Elisa knew she looked nice, but she was far too warm.

She wished she had brought along some needlework to pass the time. Mama was teaching her to make cross-stitch napkin rings. As it was, she didn't have anything to do besides eat nuts, and she was starting to feel that she'd eaten too many of those already.

"Okay, my little chipmunk," Papa said as he looked over at Elisa, her cheeks full of cashews. "We can go now."

Papa closed the big ledger and put his goose quill pen into the inkwell. Elisa noticed he faltered a bit as he stood, pulling himself up by the arms of his chair. She wondered if he was having another "weak spell" as Mama called them.

Elisa jumped down from the chair and pulled the back of her skirt away from her damp, sweaty legs. It would feel good to be outside again. The only bad thing about being in her father's office on the weekend was that very few of the big windows were open to let in the breeze.

Papa walked slowly to the wooden hat rack in the corner and claimed his new white Panama hat. Elisa thought it was by far the most handsome hat he had ever owned. When it was in place on his head, set at just the right angle, it made her father's eyes look as blue as the ocean the family was soon to cross.

Papa reached out to Elisa and she put her small hand in his big, strong one. She ran her other hand along the top of the cool marble desk for the last time as they moved toward the door. Elisa thought her father lingered a bit longer than usual before pulling the door closed and turning the big key in the keyhole. *Does he find it hard to leave his stately office knowing it won't be his much longer?* Elisa wondered.

Once they were out on the street, Papa seemed to have more energy. He swung Elisa's hand in his. The cool breeze from the harbor felt wonderful and carried the fragrance of laurel blossoms blended with the pungent, fishy smells of the day's catch.

Crossing over the bridge near Papa's office building where the street vendors sold their wares, Papa gave Elisa a coin for candy. She bought one of the *bolas quemada*, balls of caramel that all the Brazilian children loved. Papa bought a jar of molasses made from sugar cane to take home to Mama.

It seemed to Elisa that Papa knew everyone they passed on the street, or at least that they knew him. He wasn't the tallest or strongest man in Pernambuco, but when Elisa looked up at him standing so straight in his pressed white suit and new Panama hat, she was sure he was the most handsome.

"Are you still hungry, Miss Bolli?" Papa teased when he saw Elisa gazing through the window of a bakery at all the pastries lined up on silver trays.

"No, Papa, I ate some nuts at your office."

Papa laughed. "I believe you ate them all, my dear—the cashews anyway. But I won't tell your mother you've spoiled your appetite for the noonday meal."

"Where are we going to shop for my special present, Papa?" Elisa asked. She skipped along to keep up with her father's graceful, long strides. They had just passed a shop with wonderful porcelain dolls in the window, and Elisa had been sure that was where her father was leading her.

"You'll soon see, daughter. You're terribly curious for a birthday girl, aren't you?"

Finally they reached the corner shop, the last one before the street turned steeply down the hill to the wharf.

"Let's stop in here just to see what they have," Papa said, and Elisa noticed a twinkle in his eye that hadn't been there before. A tiny silver bell tinkled as Elisa and Papa stepped inside the small shop. Elisa looked around to see leather-bound books lining the walls all the way up to the ceiling. She took a deep breath to take in the wonderful, intoxicating aroma of new paper and leather.

"Oh, Papa, we've come to the bookstore!" she exclaimed. "I wish I could stay here until I read every single book."

"Bonjour, Monsieur Bolli," the shopkeeper said. Although the people of Pernambuco spoke Portuguese, the most educated also spoke French. Since they knew Elisa's father was French, many addressed him in his own language.

"Good day, Henri," Papa said. "Has my package from Paris arrived?"

"It has indeed, sir. Came in with a shipment delivered from the wharf just two days ago."

"None too soon," Papa said. "It's a birthday gift for my second daughter Elisa here. She's turning eleven this week and deserves something very special, so we've come to fetch it."

"Yes, sir. Allow me to bring it out for you," the shopkeeper said.

Elisa's heart was beating so hard she thought she would

faint. She looked up into Papa's face. He looked down at her and smiled and Elisa could tell he was almost as excited about her gift as she was.

"Papa, my special gift is from Paris?" Elisa exclaimed. "What is it?"

"Something I hope you will cherish all your life, Elisa."

Elisa had been born in Paris in 1842, but she had lived in Brazil since she was four years old, so she didn't really remember much about France. She only knew that the very finest things came from Paris. It was in Paris that Papa bought the rosepoint lace used to make a veil for his French-speaking Swiss bride, Elisa's mother, when the two were married in Lausanne, Switzerland.

Each Christmas, all the Bolli children anxiously awaited Grandfather Bolli's box from Paris. He sent wonderful books, games, elegant dresses, and dolls with wax heads, curly hair, and eyes that would open and shut. Tucked in among the tissue-paper bundles the children would find creamy chocolates and other fancy candies.

Elisa also loved the two globes that Grandfather Bolli had sent from Paris—one terrestrial and one celestial. It was because of those beautiful globes that she loved geography. So anything from Paris held a special charm for Elisa and the other children of Elise and Edouard Bolli.

Elisa thought the shopkeeper would never return with Papa's package for her. Soon she heard the sound of his footsteps approaching and he emerged from behind the cream-colored curtain that divided the front part of the shop from the storage room.

In his hands was a small package, but Elisa still didn't know what her gift was because the package was wrapped in brown paper and tied with string.

"Shall we have a look at it?" Papa teased.

"Yes. Let's!" Elisa exclaimed.

The shopkeeper took a knife and cut the string carefully

in two places. Slowly, very slowly it seemed to Elisa, he unwrapped the brown paper.

Elisa was up on her toes at this point, her hands clutching the edge of the counter and her eyes as round as the face of the mantel clock in Papa's office. Then she saw it—the most elegant brown leather Bible in the world.

"Oh, Papa! It's so beautiful!" she exclaimed. "Is it really mine?"

"Yes, honey. Your mother and I thought it was time for you to have a Bible of your own. This one is written in French. I know you've learned to speak and read Portuguese since you've lived here, but French is your native language—one that will serve you better once we are united with our French-Swiss relatives in America. We want you to have it for your birthday so you can practice your French. But more importantly, so that you will learn the truth God reveals to us through His Word and bury it deep within your heart."

The Bolli children attended an Episcopal church with their parents each Sunday, but there was no Sunday School for them to attend. It was at home that they heard the Bible stories and Scripture verses that encouraged them to live every day as children of the King. Elisa knew her father valued the Holy Bible far above all other books, because it was the inspired Word of God.

Papa handed the shopkeeper several large bills and the shopkeeper moved to his cash register to make change. Elisa reached up and gently touched the front cover of the Bible, letting her fingers move lightly over the raised filigree border and letters.

"It's the most wonderful gift ever, Papa, and I promise I'll cherish it forever," Elisa said.

"Just as I'll cherish you, precious daughter," Papa said. "Just as I'll cherish you."

Chapter Two

The shopkeeper rewrapped the Bible in the brown paper and handed it to Elisa. Because it was small, the Bible was almost as thick as it was wide. It looked like a small jewelry box when it was wrapped. Elisa carried the package to the door of the shop, but then gave it to her father to carry for fear she might drop it on the way home.

Elisa almost floated down the sidewalk. In fact, she was so full of joy that she might have floated completely away if her father hadn't been holding her hand. Her mind was full of questions as she glanced again and again in the direction of the Bible to make sure her father still had it.

Where should she keep it so the smaller children in the family wouldn't tear the pages? What should she read first? The story of David and Goliath, or the Psalms her mother always read aloud while the girls worked on their embroidery samplers in the evening?

"What do you think I should read first, Papa?" Elisa asked. "Should I begin in Genesis and read straight through?"

"That's always a good idea, Elisa, because it helps you understand God's plan for His people throughout time. However, it's the Gospel story I want you to know the best. Why don't you begin with Matthew, Mark, Luke, or John?"

"Okay, Papa! I'll read them all!" Elisa exclaimed as the two of them turned into Rua D'Aurora, the street where they lived.

"Are you feeling all right, Papa?" Elisa asked when she noticed her father seemed a bit short of breath.

"I'm fine, dear. Go on ahead. I'll be along soon."

Elisa let go of Papa's hand and ran down the lane toward the big brick house that was home to the Swiss Consul and his family.

In the front courtyard her little sister Adele, the youngest of the five Bolli children, was chasing a calico cat through the trellis-covered garden. Close behind her was the children's nursemaid, Maria. Adele had taken a bad fall off a stone wall when the family was on vacation at their country house several summers ago. Everyone was just a bit more careful of her since her long convalescence.

"Adele, Papa bought me a beautiful French Bible!" Elisa called out as she picked up her little sister under the arms and began swinging her around. "Dear me, Miss Elisa! Do be careful with her," Maria exclaimed.

"Sorry, Maria. I'm just so excited I have to tell everyone. Do you know where Mama is? And where's Cecile?"

"Everyone's inside," Maria explained. "The packing materials arrived and your mother is beginning to pack. I should be helping, but I can't just yet."

The embassy provided three black servants for the Bolli family.

Sabino was a young man with tattoos on his face and arms. He went to market, carried wood and water, mopped the floors, and ran errands.

Josepha, the big ebony cook, ruled the kitchen that occupied most of the third floor of the house. She also oversaw the pantry where all the china and crystal that the Bollis needed to entertain was displayed on wide wooden shelves.

But as the children's nursemaid, it was Maria, a young woman with skin the color of coffee with cream, who would miss the family more than anyone. It was hard for her to help with the packing when she didn't want the children to leave at all.

Elisa set Adele down carefully and then ran into the house. She passed between the bathroom and storeroom on the first floor. Then she took the stairs two at a time until she arrived on the second floor where the bedrooms, parlor, and dining room were. A large veranda off the parlor looked toward the sea. Another, off the dining room, overlooked the garden where pomegranate, fig, and laurel trees created a canopy over the grapevines, roses, and camellias.

Elisa found her mother in the parlor leaning over a large wooden barrel.

"Mama! Papa gave me the Bible! It's so beautiful, Mama. I know it's from you too. Thank you so much."

"You're very welcome, Elisa," Mama said as she straightened up and tucked a strand of loose brown hair back into the bun on the back of her head. "I know you will take very good care of it—and it will reveal God's truth to you."

Elisa stood with her arms around her mother's slender waist and looked up into the pretty face and dark brown eyes that she loved so much. She told her mother all about her morning with Papa and the wonderful bookstore with all the leather-bound books.

"Happy Birthday, dear girl," Mama said at last as she gave Elisa a kiss on the forehead. "Now, it's time we started thinking about getting packed for our move to America. Cecile, Albertine, and Emmanuel are already in their rooms sorting through their things, and Maria has promised to help Adele with hers later. You need to go to your room and begin to decide what to pack. Remember, we can't take everything."

"I will, Mama, I promise—but first I want to read my Bible," Elisa said. Just then Papa entered the room with the prized package under his arm. Elisa ran to retrieve it from him.

"One hour, then we'll eat, and then you really must get busy packing," Mama said.

"Yes, Mama, I promise," Elisa said. She carried her Bible out onto the veranda and nestled into the cushion of a large cane chair. She could hear the pigeons cooing in the pigeon roost below the veranda as she opened the Bible for the first time.

The feel of the smooth white pages under her fingers was just as wonderful as Elisa had imagined it would be. Carefully, she turned the pages one by one, moving quickly through the Old Testament but slowing down once she got to the Gospels.

Elisa was aware of the sounds of packing going on behind her in the house. Still, the family activity seemed far away from the place where she dwelled with her Bible and the Gospel according to Matthew. The French words were a bit strange at first because she was used to reading Portuguese, but the story was familiar. Soon Elisa was able to make out almost every sentence.

Distracted at one point when she heard her mother calling for Cecile, Elisa stopped reading to listen to all the activity in the house. She could almost forget the family was packing to go to America. After all, this was the time of year they would usually be packing to go to a country house for several weeks.

Cecile, fourteen, Emmanuel, twelve and the only boy, Elisa, eleven, and Albertine, ten, all had wonderful memories of the summers they spent at the country houses in the forests of Brazil. Even little Adele, seven, didn't remember the bad fall she took as clearly as she remembered chasing the plentiful butterflies through the orange groves and coffee trees.

The family would travel up the river in a narrow, long canoe pushed with a pole or go through the woods in a carriage, arriving at one of the one-story houses with porticoes made of brick and inlaid with colorful tiles.

Elisa liked swimming best of all. All the children could swim and dive and spent hours by the river each day. Using a flat willow basket for a sieve, they would catch minnows and crabs in the corners of the bathhouse, which was built half in the river, half on dry land. When the river was low they would wade across, but when the tide was high it was too dangerous to venture outside the bathhouse. All around were large vine-covered trees dipping their branches into the water.

"What are you doing daydreaming out here, Sis?" Emmanuel asked when he discovered Elisa on the veranda.

"I'm looking at my new Bible. See?"

"That's pretty nice for someone so likely to spill something on it," he said as he straightened the suspenders on his pants and tossed his dark hair out of his eyes in a way Elisa might have found charming if he hadn't been her brother.

"I won't spill anything on this, Em. I was also thinking about how much I'm going to miss going to the country house this year. Remember the time you and I took a skiff out into the river all by ourselves, and someone had to rescue us?"

"Sure, I remember. It was your idea, but Papa decided I should have been more responsible because I'm older. I got the switching of my life. I couldn't sit down for a week."

"I remember," Elisa said with a giggle. "I'm sorry about that, but it was fun, wasn't it? I still remember how it felt to dip my hand in the cool water and watch the ripples."

"You don't sound sorry," Emmanuel said as he pretended to tip Elisa's chair back to dump her out of it.

"Stop! You're going to break the chair!" Elisa squealed.

"Well, I'm sure you'll get me into more trouble in America, Lizzie," Emmanuel said. "There may not be as many spiders and lizards for you to set loose in my room, or monkeys for you to give my clothes to at the bathhouse, but I'm sure there are animals in America that you can use to torture me."

Emmanuel was the closest in age to Elisa but quite a bit larger. Because she tended to be more of a tomboy than the other girls, he was also her favorite playmate on those long summer days in the country.

"I hear there are black bears," she said mockingly.

"I'm sure if there are you'll stir them up," Emmanuel teased. "And I'll be the one who winds up climbing a tree to get away from them."

Just then Cecile and Albertine came out on the verandah.

"Mama says it's time for you to come in to eat, Elisa. Then you have to help me pack up the linens," Cecile announced. "Oh, what a gorgeous Bible."

"I got it for my birthday," Elisa said as she held the Bible out for her big sister to see.

"Well, let's take it in the house for now, Elisa. I'll look at it tonight. We have work to do."

That afternoon the two girls knelt on the floor of the dining room sorting through the damask and lace linens that they needed to pack. Even Albertine, a bit pudgier and usually a bit shyer than the other girls, was excited by the move. She tried to balance herself on top of the piles of linens until her big sisters shooed her away.

"Oh, look at this, Cile," Elisa exclaimed suddenly. "This is too lovely to be a tablecloth. What is it?"

"Let's see. Oh, that's mother's wedding veil," Cecile replied. "Remember, she showed it to us once after she had loaned it to a bride at the church. Isn't it beautiful?"

"I'd forgotten just how beautiful," Elisa said. "It's the most delicate lace I've ever seen. Far prettier than the lace Maria and her friends make with their bobbins and round cushions. Do you think Mama will mind if I try it on?"

"I'm sure she won't," Cecile replied in her older-and-wiser big sister voice. She had the same brown hair and eyes as Elisa, but was a good three inches taller. And she enjoyed being in charge when Mama wasn't around. "Just be careful with it, Elisa," Cecile said. "Papa bought it in Paris, you know."

Elisa carefully carried the veil into the dressing room outside of her parents' bedroom. The veil was over seven feet long and a foot-and-a-half wide. Handmade of rosepoint lace, the center design showcased large roses. Two rows of smaller lace roses ran all around the border. The smaller roses created the "points" that gave the lace its name.

Gently, Elisa unfolded the veil until she found the end that was gathered and stitched to a large silver comb.

16

Standing in front of the oval full-length mahogany mirror, Elisa pushed the comb into the top of her hair. The lace fell softly around her shoulders and cascaded onto the floor. Slowly she turned from side to side, then to get a better view, she climbed up on one of the trunks Mama was in the process of packing. She felt just like a fairy princess.

"Well, aren't you going to be a pretty bride," Mama said when she came into the dressing room. She carried some bed linens that belonged to the consulate, and so needed to be put away rather than packed. "I just hope I still have a few more years to wait before I see you wearing that veil down the aisle of our new church in America."

"You mean I will wear it when I get married?" Elisa asked.

"It's my dream for all of you girls to wear it," Mama said. "I just pray you will each be as happily married as I have been these past seventeen years."

Elisa thought she saw tears in her mother's eyes as she turned to put the linens into the armoire.

"Now, please find a safe place to pack that before you tear a hole in the lace, dear," Mama said. Elisa noticed that her mother lifted the corner of her apron to her eyes as she hurried from the room.

Chapter Three

Elisa's birthday celebration was held a few days later, on May 18, 1853. She received other gifts from the family, but none as precious as the French Bible.

The house was in disarray as the packing continued. At last, the day of departure arrived. On June 4, 1853, the family set sail from Pernambuco for Philadelphia.

Whereas many immigrants to America were crowded into cabins with other families or tossed about in steerage, the consulate assisted the Bolli family in booking a more comfortable passage. They set sail on a ship named the *John Farnum*, and they were the only passengers on board besides the crew.

The trip took over a month. On board, the girls did their needlework, and everyone did a lot of reading and dreaming about life in America. Papa spent most of his time resting in his berth, while Mama gathered the children on deck and read to them from *Swiss Family Robinson* to give them an adventurous spirit.

"Will we be shipwrecked and get to live in a tree like the Robinson family did when we get to America?" little Adele asked. The older children laughed along with Mama when she explained that would not be the case, but they had been wondering the same thing!

After they got over being seasick the first few days of the voyage, Elisa and her brother and sisters were allowed to eat all of the ship's stock of oranges that they wanted. They enjoyed feeding bits of orange to a Portuguese-speaking parrot named Columbo. This entertainment, plus the fun of watching the crew hoist the sails and move the giant anchors, gave them plenty to do.

Elisa read her new Bible every day—especially the Psalms that talked about God's mighty ocean. When she watched the waves crashing against the sides of the ship, she drew great comfort from the verse in Psalm 139 that read, "If I take the wings of the morning, and dwell in the uttermost parts of the sea; Even there shall thy hand lead me."

"There's no reason for us to be afraid of the unknown as long as we remember that God is in control," Mama reassured the children again and again.

"The Lord on high is mightier than the noise of many waters, yea, than the mighty waves of the sea," Elisa read in Psalm 93. Committing this verse to memory, she whispered it to comfort her little sisters in their cabin at night when they were awakened by the tossing of the ship.

"Mama, tell us again why we're going to America," Albertine said one sunny afternoon when Mama and the girls were on deck gazing out at the rolling waves.

"Papa wants us to be near my French-Swiss relatives in Tennessee in case something should happen to him," Mama said. "We aren't going back to Switzerland because there are really very few of my relatives left there. Because of the persecution of those who believe as we do, most have gone to the new country."

Mama went on to explain why the Bollis would not have been free to practice their faith in Switzerland.

"The National Protestant Church is run by the government now. Like my relatives, Papa and I believe that living by the laws of God as taught in the Bible is more important than living by the laws of man, but the government doesn't seem to understand that."

Mama didn't tell the children everything she knew about the persecution. In letters from Switzerland, she read that relatives holding Bible studies in their homes had been dragged into the streets and beaten by the authorities. Such Assemblies of the Open Brethren were not permitted, and so Edouard and Elise Bolli could not return to Switzerland with their children.

Going back to Switzerland would not have been easier for the children anyway. They had been to Switzerland, but because their father was Swiss Consul to Brazil, they had never lived there. Although the language would have been easier for them because they could have abandoned Portuguese for the French they also knew, the country would have been as unfamiliar to them as America. Only the eastern coastline of Brazil felt like home.

Papa always led the family in studying the truth of the Scripture. One night, when he was feeling stronger than he had for a few days, he gathered the whole family into a cabin below deck and read to them by candlelight from the family Bible.

Elisa followed along in her own Bible, as Papa read in Romans, chapter 10: "That if thou shalt confess with thy mouth the Lord Jesus, and shalt believe in thine heart that God hath raised him from the dead, thou shalt be saved. For with the heart man believeth unto righteousness; and with the mouth confession is made unto salvation."

"Believing in Jesus Christ is the only way to have assurance of salvation," Papa explained. "We do what the Bible instructs out of love for the Lord, but it's what we believe that saves us, not what we do."

In conversations the children had with their mother, it was more the sadness in her eyes than the words she spoke that made them wonder if Papa was even more ill than they thought.

The oldest children, Cecile, Emmanuel, and Elisa, watched their father carefully for signs of illness. He continued to be weak and short of breath, and sometimes he clutched his chest and seemed to be in pain. All the children noticed that Papa stayed in his berth more each day. Still, they couldn't begin to imagine life without their dear Papa—in America or anywhere!

Even on evenings when Papa did not feel like having dinner, the family would dine in the ship's dining room. Mama always had the place of honor next to the ship's captain.

The captain, Mr. Cook, was pleasant for a seafaring man and had great fun with the children. He was a very tall man who leaned way over from the waist to talk to the children when he saw them on deck. When he smiled at them he showed all his teeth, including a gold one that gleamed in the sunlight. His eyebrows were so bushy, Elisa thought it looked like he had a hairbrush glued to his forehead when he squinted. Most days, he was dressed in a starched white uniform with gold buttons and trim.

"I spied you mateys watching the pilot today," he said to Elisa and Emmanuel one night at dinner. "Glad to know you're paying attention in case I have to ask you to pilot the ship."

Elisa was glad Captain Cook didn't mind that the children spent long hours watching the pilot at the helm. They also loved to watch the sailor up on the mast looking through his spyglass. "Do you see land yet?" they called up to him at least twice a day. All these activities helped the days spent at sea go by faster.

The day the ship neared the equator, Captain Cook called the children to him and told them to look into his telescope.

"See if you can see the equator in there," he instructed. "We're about to cross it, you know."

Elisa peeked in first. There was definitely a line across the center of the lens, but she didn't think it was the equator. The captain laughed as all the Bolli children took turns looking into the telescope. To tease them, he had put a hair across the lens hoping to make them think they were really seeing the line they were about to cross. They did cross the equator on their journey, but the line was not really visible.

Fresh fish were often served when the family joined the

captain for dinner—fish the sailors caught with a hook and line. Imitating the sailors, Emmanuel and Elisa tried bending pins into hooks, attaching them to strings, and fastening them to the ship's railing in hopes of catching fish.

"I think I have a big one!" Elisa squealed to Emmanuel during one of their fishing efforts.

"Elisa, it's only a glob of seaweed," Emmanuel said when he helped her pull her catch over the ship's railing.

Elisa saved a sample of the seaweed pressed between the pages of a book.

Day after day, the family and their vessel sailed north through the Atlantic Ocean as they made their way from the easternmost point of South America, Pernambuco, to the northeastern shore of the United States. At long last, the children heard the sailor on watch yelling, "Land ho!" and they all ran to the railing to see the coastline of America in the distance.

* * *

On July 18, 1853, the *John Farnum* was towed from the Atlantic coast up the Delaware River to Philadelphia. The children waved wildly at passengers on other boats and saw flags of many nations waving in the summer breeze.

The first three days the Bollis spent in America they stayed in a boarding house near the home of one of Mama's cousins, Samuel Mange, and his family in Philadelphia.

There were three daughters and a son in the Mange family, and the boy was named after William Penn, the founder of Pennsylvania. At dinner, Mr. Mange gave the Bolli children a history lesson, interjecting as much French as he could to help them understand his account of all the historic sites in and around the city.

Elisa thought it was funny that Mr. and Mrs. Mange insisted on referring to their son by his full name, but after she learned more about the Quaker William Penn who established the colony of Pennsylvania in 1682, she understood their pride.

"Please pass me the huckleberry jam," William Penn Mange, who was more interested in eating than in hearing about his namesake, said to Elisa.

Elisa looked around the table, but she had never seen jam made of huckleberries in beet sugar before. She had never seen sweet churned butter, either. She stared at both of the small crystal bowls wondering which one to pass. Finally, one of the Mange sisters reached around to get the jam, sparing Elisa any further embarrassment.

When the family had a chance to see the historic sights in Philadelphia the next day, Elisa was glad Mr. Mange had told them something of the city's history. They saw Independence Hall, the very place where the Declaration of Independence was signed, and stood by the grave of founding father Benjamin Franklin at Christ Church.

"Was that really the Liberty Bell we saw?" Emmanuel asked at dinner the next night. "I thought it would be so much larger."

Elisa and Cecile couldn't stop thinking about the house where Betsy Ross sewed the first American flag. When they climbed the narrow stairs to their attic room in the boarding house that night, they unpacked their samplers and pretended that they were Betsy—stitching by candlelight to get the flag ready in time.

The children were also fascinated with the more modern sights of the city. The ships in the port weren't unlike the ones they were used to seeing in Pernambuco, but the huge department stores seemed like giant treasure chests the girls couldn't wait to explore.

When the family went on shopping excursions in the city, Papa stayed behind to rest. Being in the marketplace without him made Elisa sad. The sights and smells of the flowers and fish made her remember all the Saturday mornings she had gone with Papa to the marketplace in Pernambuco.

"Papa, we saw the most beautiful gold watches in the

jewelry store window," Elisa ran to tell him after one shopping trip. "And the diamond rings! Oh, Papa! They are even more dazzling than the ones in the stores in Pernambuco!"

*   *   *

After three days, the family left Philadelphia on a large steamer and went to Charleston, South Carolina, then on to Savannah, Georgia. In Savannah they boarded a train, the first train the children had ever seen, and rode all the way to Loudon, Tennessee. From the train windows they took in the rolling green hills, the rivers, and the trees of East Tennessee. In the distance, a hazy blue mountain range reminded Elisa of a rumpled comforter on an unmade bed.

The conductor took Emmanuel with him to collect the tickets from passengers on the other cars.

"There are so many cars I lost count of them," he told the girls breathlessly when he got back to his seat. "And you should see how much coal they have to shovel into the big steam engines."

From Loudon, the travel-weary family took a stagecoach to Knoxville, Tennessee, where they spent the first night in the Lamar House on Gay Street.

"Is this our new home?" little Adele asked Elisa as she lifted her sleepy, blonde head off her sister's shoulder and saw the fancy chandelier in the foyer.

"No, silly girl," Elisa laughed. "This is a boarding house. We'll only be here one night."

The next day, the Bollis, along with all their trunks and other belongings, moved in with the Esperandieus, a French-Swiss family who had settled on a farm at Third Creek near Knoxville four years earlier. Mrs. Esperandieu was a first cousin of Mama's, but the Bolli children called her "aunt" and her husband, Reverend Esperandieu, "uncle" as was the Swiss custom. The Esperandieus had five children—Lily, Mary, Adele, Berthe, and Frederick.

*   *   *

The Bollis spent almost a month with the Esperandieus. The children loved exploring the farm with their cousins. And the cousins were pleased to help Cecile, Emmanuel, Elisa, Albertine, and Adele learn English as they played together on the farm. The teaching and the learning were both made easier because all the children spoke French.

Mama and Papa had a lot to learn too. Although the terrain in East Tennessee was not completely unlike what they remembered of Switzerland, they knew nothing about the farming life they seemed destined to have. While the children played and learned English from their cousins, Mama spent long hours in the kitchen with Aunt Esperandieu learning how to put up produce for the winter.

Papa learned about the laws of property ownership from Uncle Esperandieu. Frequently, he would borrow the Esperandieus' wagon to go looking for land or to run an errand in town. Elisa and Cecile would ride along whenever they could.

"May we go with you, Papa?" Elisa asked one day when she noticed her father hitching a horse to the wagon.

"You don't even know where I'm going!" Papa teased. "Hop in. I'm just going out to look at some land. You girls may go if you promise to practice your English with me as we ride along."

Eagerly Elisa and Cecile scrambled into the back of the wagon. They had hoped for a chance to chatter together in French or Portuguese since they were alone together, but Papa didn't want to miss an opportunity for all of them to learn.

"All right, girls," he said. "I want you to give me the English name of everything we pass along the way."

"Maple tree," Cecile called out.

"Born!" Elisa said, and wondered why Cecile and her father dissolved in laughter.

"I believe it's *barn*, dear," Papa said at last. And so it went all afternoon.

On the way back to the Esperandieu farm, the girls noticed that their father was barely able to sit up and steer the wagon. When they pulled up to the house, he called for Emmanuel to come help him down and tend to the horse.

"I had hoped Papa was just tired from our trip from Brazil," Cecile said to Elisa when the two sat on the front porch snapping beans for dinner, "but he doesn't seem to be getting stronger."

"I know, Cile," Elisa said. "Do you think we'll be able to stay in Tennessee if Papa doesn't get well enough to work again?"

"We came here so Mama's relatives could help us, Elisa, so yes, we could stay. But it's too soon to worry about that. We just have to keep praying that Papa will get better soon."

During the month the Bollis spent with the Esperandieus, Elisa's mother was reconnected with all her relatives from Canton de Vaud in Switzerland. No reunion was sweeter than that of Mama with her sister, Cecile Chavannes, who had moved from Switzerland with her husband Theodore Chavannes just a few years before to settle on his parents' farm. Whenever the Bolli children couldn't find their mother at any of the big family gatherings, they knew she was with Aunt Cecile. Sure enough, they would find the two sisters huddled together in a corner someplace talking, laughing, and hugging one another until it was time to go home.

Five families of French-Swiss had come to Tennessee in 1849 to escape religious persecution, joining three families already in residence. By the time the Bollis arrived in 1853, more families were joining this new colony of immigrants each year. The Bolli children were surrounded by caring aunts and uncles and many fun-loving cousins.

The welcome celebrations went on for days. Every meal the families shared was full of stories of their passages, introductions to their children and spouses, and the warm feeling of love and acceptance that makes a place soon feel like home.

"If only Papa wasn't sick, everything would be wonderful here," Elisa whispered to Cecile one night as the two of them snuggled in bed together.

Soon Papa purchased a 265-acre farm a mile west of the Esperandieus. The farm included a large two-story frame house, a smaller log house, and stables.

Finally it was moving day again, but this time the Bollis were moving into their own farmhouse. There would be no servants in this home, and Papa had still not recovered from the trip and spent most of the day in bed. That left Mama and the children to do most of the moving in themselves.

"Elisa, you're not holding your end up," Cecile complained as she and her sister struggled to get one of the trunks up the front stairs of the farmhouse that would be their new home.

"I can't even see my feet, Cile," Elisa said. "How can I tell if I'm holding the trunk up or not?"

At last, everything was in the house.

"I know we don't have many places to store things," Mama told the girls. "Just unpack what you can, and I'll ask Emmanuel to carry the rest of the boxes up to the attic."

Almost all the family's furniture had been left in Brazil, including the fine mahogany tables, the mirrors, the piano, and the heavy iron bedsteads. But the farmhouse had several built-in cupboards, and the other families brought over any furniture they could spare. Soon the unpacking was done.

Chapter Four

A few weeks after the move, Mama began thinking about the lace veil she had worn on her wedding day. Although it was only a piece of cloth, to her it had always symbolized hope for the future. She had left so many pretty things behind in Brazil, and with her husband ill and unable to work, she didn't know if the family would ever be able to replace all they had lost. At least there was the veil.

"Elisa! Didn't you pack my lace wedding veil in Pernambuco? I haven't seen it since we moved. Please go into the attic and find it for me," she called upstairs.

"Sure, Mama," Elisa answered, not knowing how difficult it would be to fulfill her mother's request.

Elisa pulled on the rope that brought the ladder to the attic down and climbed up through the opening. She quickly located the trunk full of linens she and Cecile had packed that sunny day in Pernambuco.

Elisa carefully lifted each piece of linen out and placed it on the floor next to her. A long lace table runner, a set of doilies—all lovely, but not what she was hoping to find. She could feel her heart beating faster the longer she searched. After all, it wasn't just any piece of lace that she hoped to see. It was her mother's wedding veil.

"Did you find it yet?" Cecile asked as she climbed up through the opening to the attic to join Elisa in the search.

"No, Cile. Don't you think I would have come back down-stairs if I had?"

"Well, I hope it's not lost. Papa gave that veil to Mama as a wedding gift. We're supposed to wear it at our weddings."

"I know," Elisa sighed, "and it's not like we could have another made. I don't think you and I can go to Paris."

Elisa and Cecile thought back to the day in Pernambuco when they had last seen the veil. They had dreamed of their own wedding days to come.

"I remember your wanting to try it on," Cecile said. "You took it into the bedroom. Then what did you do with it?"

"That's what I can't remember, Cile. Mama said to pack it somewhere safe, and I thought I did, but I don't remember where."

The two girls went through all the linens again. Then they sat on the attic floor and looked at one another somberly.

"Why can't I remember where I packed the veil, Cile?" Elisa said. She felt the tears brimming up in her eyes. "Was I just too excited about my birthday and our move to be thinking clearly? If only I could remember."

Just then Albertine and Adele called up from the bottom of the ladder.

"Lizzie! Cile! We want to play in the attic too," Albertine called out.

"Come help us climb the ladder!" Adele added.

"No, girls," Cecile replied. "We're not playing, we're looking for something. We'll be down in a few minutes. Quiet now. Papa is resting."

"The veil isn't in the trunk, Lizzie," Cecile said, turning back to her sister. "We might as well go back downstairs."

Elisa let the tears spill down her face and didn't even bother to wipe them away.

"I know, Lizzie. We'll pray about it," Cecile said at last. "We don't know where the veil is, but the Lord does. Papa said that the Lord brought us to this place. He brought all our trunks and belongings, too. He'll help us find the veil. Here, use this handkerchief from the trunk. Let's pray."

"All right, Cile. I'll start," Elisa said. She wiped her eyes and bowed her head. "Oh gracious Lord, you protected us as we sailed across the ocean. You have kept our father alive even though he is so sick. You helped us find a place to live in our new country. Help us now, Lord."

"If it be Your will," Cecile added, "let us find the veil. It would make Mama so happy, Lord, and you know how tired she is now. You know where the veil is. Please help us find it."

Cecile put her arm around Elisa and added, "In Jesus' precious name we pray. Amen." She gave her younger sister a hug. "I feel better, Lizzie, don't you?"

"I guess so, Cile," Elisa said, as she wiped a few more tears from her cheeks. "Will you go with me to tell Mama I couldn't find the veil?"

"Sure. She's in the kitchen making soup for Papa. Come on. No more tears. Remember, we prayed."

The kitchen was on the bottom floor of the two-story frame house. Since it was in the back of the house, the kitchen window looked out across the rolling Tennessee fields. When the girls arrived at the door of the kitchen they saw their mother gazing out the window at the huge old maple and walnut trees that dappled the backyard.

Mama stood peeling potatoes and carrots to cream into a soft but nourishing soup for her ailing husband. The girls knew there would be plenty for them too. With five children to feed in addition to Papa, Mama would make at least two kettles full.

Elisa grabbed Cecile by the skirt just before the girls got to the kitchen door and pulled her back out into the hall.

"Are you sure we have to tell her, Cile?" Elisa asked. "Mama's been working so hard, and I think she's really worrying about Papa. Did you see how she was just staring out into the backyard?"

Both of the older girls were sensitive to their mother's feelings. Although she never complained, Mama sometimes talked about the days in Brazil when they had all their furniture and pretty things.

"It was wonderful having the servants to help with all the cooking and cleaning," Mama said one day. "But you know what I miss most about Brazil? Sending your father off to his day's work and watching him walk through the front garden in his handsome white suit and Panama hat—then welcoming him home at the end of the day."

Of course, that was before Papa's heart started growing weaker day by day.

The children never heard their mother criticize her husband's decision to bring the family to Tennessee, and they knew she had been very happy to see her sister and cousins. But when they saw her staring out the kitchen window like she was doing, it was almost as if she were trying to see all the way back to Pernambuco—to see the life they had lived in sun-baked days there.

"Don't you think she's going to ask if you found the veil?" Cecile said. "Come on, I'll help you tell her."

The girls came into the kitchen and sat down at the big wooden table. Mama put down the paring knife she was using and turned to face them. "What is it?" she asked. "You girls look like you've seen a ghost in the attic."

"It isn't what we saw that has upset us, Mama," Elisa began. "It's what we didn't see." Elisa kicked her sister gently under the table.

"We didn't find the veil, Mama," Cecile said. "Lizzie looked through the trunk of linens twice, but it's just not there."

Their mother turned her face toward the kitchen window again.

"She isn't saying anything at all," Elisa whispered to Cecile. "Why doesn't she say something?"

"Shhh . . . maybe she's trying to decide what to say," Cecile said. "Just wait."

"Well, we'll have more time to look another day," Mama turned to say at last. "Maybe it's in another trunk. You know girls, it's only a veil . . . but oh the memories it brings back of the July morning in 1836 when I married your father."

"Tell us about the wedding again, Mama!" Elisa exclaimed. The girls never tired of hearing about the romance between their mother and father, and the story of the wedding day was their favorite part.

Mama wiped her hands and joined the girls at the kitchen table.

"All the family in Lausanne, including many of the aunts and uncles now here with us in Tennessee, had gathered to wish us well," she began. "I remember walking across the stones of the courtyard outside the Cathedral of Lausanne in my white lace dress with the veil Papa brought from Paris billowing all around me."

"Remember to tell us what Papa was wearing," Elisa said.

"Oh, yes. He was very handsome in a dark gray suit with a starched white shirt. The suit coat had tails, and he wore a black-striped, silk cravat from Paris," Mama said. "My bouquet was made of edelweiss, roses, and daisies, and Papa had a sprig of edelweiss in his lapel as a boutonniere."

"And you were nervous to be marrying Papa, right Mama?" Cecile asked.

"Yes, a bit," Mama said, "because I didn't really know him very well yet. If you remember, I met Papa through Theodore Chavannes. After he married my sister, Cecile, the two of them decided Papa and I should meet."

"And when you met Papa, did you fall very much in love, Mama?" Elisa asked, knowing full well the answer her mother would give.

"From my head to my toes. I knew I loved him and that he loved me. I just didn't know what the future would hold for us. But because I knew Papa had given his life to Jesus Christ just as I had, I was able to put it all in the Lord's hands."

"I like that part, Mama," Cecile said.

Just then Emmanuel came through the back door into the kitchen, with Albertine and Adele close behind him. With Papa sick in bed, most of the chores of running the farm were falling to Emmanuel. Fortunately, all the uncles and cousins were willing to help. They taught Emmanuel how to harvest the vegetables the previous owners had planted and tend to the chickens.

"Uncle Theodore's dog had a litter of eight puppies," Emmanuel said as he drew water from the kitchen pump to wash his hands.

"We want a puppy, Mama!" Albertine squealed.

"May we have one, Mama? Please?" Adele chirped in.

"A puppy? I don't know about that," Mama replied.

"Adele and I will take care of it ourselves," Albertine said. "We help Emmanuel with all his chores now. I know we can take care of a puppy. May we have one, Mama?"

Emmanuel laughed at Albertine's report that the younger girls were a help with the chores. He knew they liked spending time with him so he took them along. But a help? Not really.

"You have to ask Papa. If he says yes, we'll have a look at them on Sunday when we go to the Chavannes farm for services," Mama said. "But we would have to wait several weeks before bringing one home."

"We know, Mama," Albertine said. "Come on, Adele, let's go talk to Papa about the puppy."

"If he's sleeping, don't wake him!" Mama called out as the girls ran from the kitchen.

"What were you three discussing so intently when we came in?" Emmanuel asked.

"I was telling the girls about the day Papa and I were married," Mama said.

"That again? Don't you girls ever get tired of hearing that story?" he teased.

"If you would let us be, we could hear the end of it, Em," Elisa said.

"I think I'll go talk to Papa too," he laughed as he followed the little girls in the direction of his parents' bedroom.

"Now, Mama, tell us. Was it hard to say good-bye to your family?" Cecile asked.

"Yes, it was. I could only imagine what it would be like to leave Switzerland for Brazil. And I certainly didn't know what would be expected of me as the wife of the Swiss Consul," Mama said. "As for America, well, I never dreamed my French groom would one day bring me here to live as well. But here we are, aren't we?"

"Oh, Mama, I know you said one glance at the veil makes you feel like a bride again. I'm so sorry I can't remember where I packed it."

"Elisa, don't go on so," Mama said as she went back to the hearth to stir the kettles of soup.

"I was hoping to see it again, because doing so seems to restore the hope in my heart. Yet I know my only real hope comes from the Lord.

"It's just a piece of cloth, isn't it?" Mama said as she rejoined the girls at the table. "It may turn up yet. If not, I'll just have to make a new veil to be our family heirloom. After all, we're in a new country, so we need new heirlooms! And I do believe I have time. You don't have a suitor to tell me about, do you, Cile?"

At her question, the girls laughed. Then they hopped up to give their mother a hug.

"No, Mama, there's no suitor yet," Cecile said between giggles. "And Lizzie doesn't have one either."

"Well then, we won't worry until we know there's a wedding on the way, will we?"

"Oh, Mama! I almost forgot," Elisa added. "We prayed about the veil. We asked the Lord to help us find it."

"Then it's out of our hands, isn't it? I have a wonderful idea to get our minds off the veil for now. Why don't you girls go in and sing to your father while I finish up supper? I know it won't be the same without the piano, but you still have your accordion, Lizzie. I put it in the bedroom. Go on now. Include Albertine and Adele. Nothing cheers Papa like his girls."

Elisa and Cecile hurried to do as their mother asked. For now, the veil was forgotten as they began planning their performance for Papa.

Chapter Five

The Bolli children loved having a chance to perform. Making up songs and playing instruments was a prime form of entertainment for them. It didn't really matter whether they had talent—the fun was in the trying. And Papa made the best audience of all.

Elisa knocked before entering her parents' bedroom.

"Entrez-vous!" Papa called out. "Whoever you are, you might as well join the merry group!"

When Elisa came in, she discovered Albertine and Adele sitting on her father's bed begging him for the puppy. Emmanuel sat in a chair nearby.

"Please, Papa," little Adele said. "Bertie and I will take care of it—we promise."

"Elisa, rescue me from these insistent beggars," Papa said. Then he laughed. "My goodness! I can't make a decision about a dog I haven't seen. So far, Em's done nothing but encourage them."

Elisa smiled at the younger girls bouncing around on her father's bed. Then she spotted her accordion on top of a trunk that was temporarily being used as a bureau.

The accordion had been Elisa's since she first started school in Brazil. Some dust from the dirt roads had come through the open windows and settled in the creases. Some of the keys were a bit loose. Still, it was the only instrument the family owned since they had to leave their piano behind in Brazil.

Elisa knew she could still create beautiful music with it. Just feeling the accordion in her hands brought back so many memories of family concerts.

"Come along, sisters," Elisa called to Albertine and Adele. "We're going to perform for Papa, but first we have to practice in the parlor."

"Certainly you have saved me, Elisa," Papa said with a wave of his hand as Albertine and Adele scrambled off the bed and ran after their big sister.

The bedroom Elisa's parents shared was on the bottom floor of the two-story house, just down the hall from the kitchen. The room was designed to be an informal drawing room, but Mama wanted Papa to be a part of the daily activity. She also wanted him close enough for her to check on him frequently during the day, so that room became their bedroom.

The big windows made this an extra cheerful room too. One where the children loved to congregate for special conversations with their father. As sad as they were that he was sick, they relished having him so available to them.

Since the largest bedroom upstairs was not being used by the master and mistress of the house, Cecile and Elisa shared it. It had one window, looking out the front of the house. From here the girls could see down the winding lane lined with maple trees that connected the property to the main road. Albertine and Adele shared another upstairs bedroom. It was on the opposite side of the house, with a window looking into the back yard.

Emmanuel could have slept in the bedroom next to Cecile and Elisa on the front of the house, but he chose to sleep on an enclosed sleeping porch next to the kitchen. He felt this location better suited his role as temporary "man of the house."

Emmanuel felt more than able and ready to protect his family and their home from any intruders—animal or human. Although he never had to use it, Papa even allowed him to keep a loaded rifle on his sleeping porch at night. He was careful to lock it in a trunk during the day.

The two-story house also had covered porches with railings on both the front and the back. Seen from the side of the house, these porches looked like bookends holding the house erect.

On the back porch were a butter churn, garden tools, baskets for harvesting, and other things the family needed.

The front porch was purely for sitting, talking, daydreaming, and watching the world go by on the road below the house. Come evening, the four large rocking chairs on the front porch were occupied by the first four residents to finish their after-supper chores. Whoever didn't get a chair took a seat on the front steps to join in the conversation.

The formal parlor where Elisa was leading her sisters to rehearse was to the right of the front foyer and had the only formal fireplace and mantel in the house. Had the drawing room been available, this parlor would have been closed and kept clean for special visitors. But since the Bollis didn't have fancy parlor furniture yet anyway, they used this room every day.

The formal dining room to the left of the foyer was almost empty too. But it was easier for the family to gather around the big wooden table in the kitchen for meals anyway. Especially since Papa didn't need a place at the table because Mama took his meals to him on a tray.

The staircase leading to the upstairs level climbed straight up from the front foyer. Under the front stairs was a cozy closet with a sloped roof. Albertine and Adele called this closet their "princess castle," and whenever they were missing at mealtime, the rest of the family knew where to find them.

Once, Bertie took one of the lighted candles the girls took up to their bedchambers at night into the closet and left it burning until morning. It burned clear down to the candleholder, and spilled tallow onto the wood floor. Mama said it was only by the grace of God that the whole house didn't burn down. After that, the girls had to crack the door to let in just enough light to see their dolls and toys.

When Elisa and the younger girls got to the parlor, Cecile was arranging all the chairs the family owned into a circle. It was obvious she had also appointed herself director of the rehearsal.

All the wooden floors in the new house were bare, so the parlor made a wonderful rehearsal hall.

"We want to sing one of the French songs Mama taught us in Pernambuco!" Albertine called out.

"I think Papa would enjoy some of the hymns we used to sing in church too," Elisa said. "They always seem to cheer him so."

"I'm sure there will be a chance to do all the songs that we want to sing," Cecile said. "After all, we have a dedicated audience. If Papa gets too tired today, we can always perform for him again tomorrow. Now, what should we sing first?"

"Let's sing 'Sur Le Point D'Avignon,'" Adele suggested. "We can hold hands to make the circle and skip around Papa's bed!"

"Papa's bedstead is up against the wall, silly," Cecile said. "But there's room at the foot of the bed for the circle. Let's give that one a try, shall we?"

"Wait, Cecile," Albertine said. "Where's Emmanuel? We need his voice for the bass harmony."

The girls all laughed at this suggestion. Since he had turned twelve, Emmanuel's voice had been changing. It might be bass when he sang, or it might be soprano. There was just no guarantee. This uncertainty made him shy about singing at all. However, Albertine found him still in Papa's room talking to Papa about the farm, and she persuaded him to join the rest of the children in the parlor.

"I'll play the first three chords as an introduction," Elisa said once the performers were assembled. "Then we'll all start singing together."

Everyone except Elisa, who was busy playing the accordion, joined hands in a circle. Skipping toward the left, they sang, "*Sur le point d'Avignon* (On the bridge of Avignon) *on y danse, on y danse* (everyone is dancing), *sur le point d'Avignon, on y danse tous en rond* (everyone is dancing in a circle)."

When it was time to change directions and skip to the right instead, there was a great deal of confusion. Finally, everyone just sat on the floor laughing.

The sound of laughter was inviting to Mama. She left the kitchen and stood at the door of the parlor wiping her hands on a towel and smiling at the giggling children. Hearing them laugh did more for her heart than anything could—anything except seeing Papa well again.

"Wait, Mama!" Elisa said. "Don't listen yet. Wait until we've practiced. We want you to be part of the audience with Papa."

All right, dear," Mama said as she turned to go back to her work.

On the second practice, the change in direction went more smoothly.

The girls stepped to the center of the circle and curtsied when the lyrics directed, "*Les jeune filles font comme çi* (The young girls go like this)." Then Emmanuel, being the only boy, stepped inside the circle and bowed to the words "*Les garçons font comme ça* (The boys go like that)."

Going through all the verses, the children had fun imitating dolls, soldiers, and even animals like gorillas and frogs in turn. When Cecile asked what other animals they wanted to make a part of the song, Adele called out "*Chien!* (dog)" and got quite a laugh from the group. Obviously, it was her way of bringing up the puppy to Papa once more.

"We really need to learn some American songs now that we live in America," Cecile said when that song was over.

"I learned one of the chanteys the sailors were singing on the ship," Albertine said. "Do you want me to teach it to you?"

"No, thank you, dear," Cecile laughed. "I don't think Papa

would be pleased to know you learned to sing like a sailor."

"Cousin Emma Chavannes could teach us some songs," Elisa said. "When she was here visiting last week she helped me bring extra water from the well in the backyard to the kitchen for Mama. As we walked together with the bucket, trying not to let too much water slosh over onto our feet, she was singing a song about 'the old oaken bucket that hangs in the well.' If only I had paid closer attention, I might have picked up the melody and the words."

The kindness Emma showed Elisa was typical of the entire Chavannes family. Mama's sister Cecile was married to Theodore Chavannes. His brother, the Reverend Adrien Chavannes and his wife, Anna, were Emma's parents. Like their other French-Swiss relatives, the Chavannes family had rallied around the Bollis to help them get settled.

As a retired minister, Reverend Chavannes was the spiritual leader of this colony of French-speaking Swiss people in America, and everyone came to him first with questions about how to accomplish all the things that needed to be done to establish homes or set up businesses.

Other families who had settled in Knox County from Switzerland included the Sterchis, the Truans, the Tauxes, and the Buffats. But of the many cousins and other children in these families, Emma was fast becoming Elisa's favorite.

Emma was a year and two months older than Elisa, but unlike some other older girls, she never flaunted the age difference. Elisa was first attracted to her because she thought she was strikingly beautiful with her long, curly dark hair, blue eyes, and her rosy cheeks with dimples. When she discovered that Emma was compassionate, affectionate, and good-humored too, she looked forward to getting to know her better.

"Well, we don't know any American songs yet," Cecile said. "But the traditional old hymns we sing at church mean the same in every language. Elisa's right about how Papa loves them. Now that he can't attend services with us, I do think we should sing hymns for him."

"Remember the solo I learned for our last service in Pernambuco?" Elisa asked. "It's a verse from 'Oh, God, Our Help in Ages Past.' I can sing that."

"I can sing 'Fairest Lord Jesus,'" Adele chirped in.

Why don't we close by singing 'Come Thou Fount of Every Blessing'?" Emmanuel contributed. "Papa loves that hymn."

"Perfect," Cecile declared. "I think we're ready. Let's go perform for Papa before it's time for supper."

Chapter Six

Soon all the noise and activity that had been in the parlor moved to Papa's bedroom. Mama was sitting next to Papa on the bed when the children entered. They set about pushing trunks and chairs up against the wall to create a stage for the performance.

"Mmmm, I smell cornbread baking," Albertine said.

"It should be ready just in time to have with our soup for dinner," Mama said. "But let's see this performance first."

It was still strange to the children for their mother to be cooking for the family. Josepha, the Bollis' cook, had been the one to put delicious meals on the table in Pernambuco. But recipe by recipe, Mama was learning to cook American style from her relatives. Cornbread made from freshly ground cornmeal and flour, and spread with homemade apple butter, was fast becoming a family favorite.

Elisa found a spot with enough elbow room to play the accordion and waited while the other children found their spots. She looked at her parents. Her father was still under the covers, his head propped up on a pillow. Mama was sitting on the bed next to Papa, leaning back with her arm across the top of his pillow. Gently she ran her fingers through her husband's blonde hair to soothe him. Both of them were bathed in the late afternoon sunlight streaming through the window.

Elisa had never seen her parents being so intimate in front of their children before. Her mother looked more at home than she had in weeks.

Soon the circling around began. Papa laughed so hard as the children went through their antics that he started coughing and couldn't stop. Mama had to bring a glass of water from the kitchen and help him sit up to sip it. Soon he was fine again, and the performance continued with Elisa's solo.

"O God, our help in ages past, our hope for years to come," Elisa sang, each note accompanied by a squeeze of the accordion. "Be thou our Guard while life shall last, and our eternal home." Did Papa have tears in his eyes, or was it just the dust from outside, or his coughing spell, that made his eyes water?

Soon it was Adele's turn to sing her solo.

"Fairest Lord Jesus," she began. "Ruler of all nations."

"No, it's nature! Ruler of all nature!" Albertine said.

"Ruler of all nature," Adele continued, "O Thou of God and ... and ... Oh, Bertie, you made me forget!" Adele cried, and she ran to bury her face in Cecile's skirt.

"It's okay, Adele," Cecile said. "We'll all sing with you."

"O Thou of God and man the Son, Thee will I cherish, Thee will I honor, Thou, my soul's Glory, Joy, and Crown."

Then Cecile asked Mama and Papa to join in to sing "Come Thou Fount of Every Blessing." Papa's singing was punctuated with coughing, but it was so good to hear his voice blending in with the family's again that the children didn't mind the interruptions. Besides, the coughs were drowned out by Emmanuel's squeaky leaps between octaves.

Elisa played as they sang. The performance ended with the last line of the second stanza: "Let that grace now, like a fetter, bind my wandering heart to Thee." Adele sang "feather" instead of "fetter," loudly enough for all to clearly hear her, so everyone else finished the stanza through stifled laughter.

"*Bravo!*" Papa said at last. "*Bravo, mes enfants!* Let us praise the Lord for this fine performance and bless the food that we are about to receive."

It was good to hear Papa pray. The children used to think his graces went on far too long when they had to smell the wonderful aromas of food without being able to eat it. But now they missed his prayers at the table.

"Lord, we thank You for the voices of these young servants of Yours," Papa prayed. "Thank You for the joy they bring to their mother and me, and keep their souls, and ours, in Your care. Now we ask You to bless this food we are about to receive. May You use it to make us strong in Your service.... In Jesus' name we pray, Amen."

The children scrambled from the room in the direction of the kitchen table. Elisa stayed behind to return the accordion to its spot on top of the trunk. She glanced at her parents once more before leaving the room. Her mother was plumping up her father's feather pillow and smoothing his coverlet one last time before going to serve supper. Then with the corner of her apron, Mama wiped away the tears that were trickling down Papa's cheek.

The kitchen was far too warm from the cooking that had been done all day. When Mama came into the kitchen, the first thing she did was open the back door to let the breeze in.

It wasn't possible to cook without heating up the kitchen, because all the country kitchens had open fireplaces rather than wood-burning stoves. The soup Mama made simmered in big iron kettles suspended over the open flame on cranes. The cornbread baked in an iron oven that was placed on live coals on the hearth. More live coals were heaped on the top of the oven so the bread baked evenly.

Emmanuel helped Mama lift the heavy lids and serve the soup. Soon a breadboard with steaming squares of cornbread was placed in the middle of the table. Everyone reached for a square at once.

Mama excused herself to take a tray to Papa, then came back to assume her spot at one end of the table. Emmanuel sat on Papa's end.

"Mama, when do you think Papa will be well enough to sit at the table and eat with us again?" Albertine asked.

Elisa felt a lump form in her throat when she realized that

the answer everyone feared, but no one dared utter, was never.

"That's in the Lord's hands, Bertie," is all Mama said after a moment's pause. "Remember to say your prayers for Papa. That's all we can do."

Elisa looked across the table at Cecile and their brown eyes locked. Even these closest of sisters hadn't allowed themselves to speak aloud to one another what their hearts feared most. The doctors Papa saw in Brazil hadn't been able to strengthen his heart and keep him from growing weaker. Dr. Clark, who rode out from Knoxville, didn't seem to be able to help him either. What if Papa never got well enough to return to the table? What if he never got well at all?

Now the soup in Elisa's bowl, the tiny pieces of carrot and potato and beef that had looked so appetizing before, had no appeal to her. Albertine's simple question had changed everything.

Elisa's thoughts went back to how different Papa had been just two months before when they had first arrived in Tennessee. He had been weak then too, but he had spent some of each day out of bed. He had even borrowed a buggy to take Elisa and Cecile to Knoxville with him so they could see the small-town sights.

Walking hand-in-hand with Papa down Gay Street, the muddy main street of town, Cecile and Elisa had listened as Papa pointed out the general merchandise stores, the courthouse spire a few blocks away, and the banks. The two girls had eaten hard candy from a crystal dish in the lobby of the Tennessee Bank, on the corner of Gay and Main, while their father finished signing some of the paperwork for purchasing the farm. Then he had treated them to ice cream at Fatio & Brothers Drugstore. How long ago that seemed now, with Papa so sick in bed day after day.

"There's plenty of cornbread," Mama said. "Another pan is still in the oven. Aren't you going to eat anything, Elisa?"

"I guess I'm not very hungry after all, Mama," Elisa said.

"I'm sorry."

"I certainly hope you aren't coming down with something, dear."

"I'm all right, Mama," Elisa said. "Why don't I clear the table for you? You've been on your feet all day."

Elisa knew there was a lot of work to be done to keep the farm and the family running smoothly. But she was beginning to worry that Mama was going to get sick too if she kept working so hard.

"Work is necessary for contentment and happiness," Mama said, repeating a piece of wisdom her mother had given her. "Rest is for the future, not the present—yet I'd be happy for you to clear the table!"

Once the dishes were dried and put back on the shelf, everyone except Papa gathered on the front porch. Mama was the last to join the group.

"Did you just tuck Papa in bed?" Adele asked.

"I went in to check on him," Mama said with a smile. "He's just fallen asleep."

"Did he say anything about the puppy before he went to sleep?" Adele asked.

"No, honey, he didn't," Mama said. She sat down in a rocking chair, pulled Adele up onto her lap, and gave her a good squeeze.

"He was too worn out by your performance to think about the puppy tonight. Maybe tomorrow."

"Look! There's a lightnin' bug!" Albertine said.

"I can catch one before you can, Bertie!" Adele said as she jumped off her mother's lap and ran down the porch steps.

No one in the Bolli family had ever seen a firefly before moving to Tennessee—not even Mama and Papa. Adele and Albertine soon loved to run barefooted in the cool evening grass chasing after them just as much as the other children of the region. They even called them "lightnin' bugs" like their neighbors.

Each time they saw another tiny light blinking in the dusk, the girls would squeal with delight and run in the bug's direction.

No sooner would they reach the spot where they saw the bug than it would zip away in the dark leaving them empty-handed. Eventually, each girl had a firefly cupped in her hands. They took turns peeking between the cracks of their fingers to see the bugs glow.

Once the girls captured about a dozen bugs in a jar like they saw the neighbor children doing. They punched holes in the jar lid so the bugs could breathe. Then they set the jar on the table between their two beds. When the room was totally dark, the bugs created a twinkling, blinking nightlight.

But the girls were upset when they woke up the next morning and discovered that all the bugs had died during the night. Now they just caught them, enjoyed the miraculous blinking for a while, and let them go again.

"How can you see what you're doing, Mama?" Elisa asked when she noticed her mother had opened the sewing basket next to the chair and was hemming one of Albertine's old dresses for Adele to wear.

"Oh, there's still a bit of light left," Mama said. "Besides, after four daughters, I do this more by feel than by sight."

Even when the family had servants doing the cleaning and cooking, Mama did most of her own sewing. She stitched beautifully, and taught her girls to make even stitches in their embroidery samplers. They tried hard to get the stitches even the first time. They knew that if they didn't, Mama would soon have them tearing out their work to begin again.

The store-bought dresses the girls brought from Brazil, especially the ones Grandfather Bolli sent from Paris, seemed out of place in the simpler lifestyle of East Tennessee. When they had first arrived, Mama asked Papa to buy a bolt of bleached domestic fabric and a bolt of calico on one of his trips to Knoxville. Each day she cut the fabric to make the undergarments, dresses, and shirts her family needed. At night, she sewed by candlelight.

Once Elisa got up to go to the outhouse in the middle of the night. She looked down the hall on her way to the back door and saw candlelight coming from her parents' bedroom. The next morning, there was a new, blue calico dress on Cecile's chair at the breakfast table—one Elisa also admired since she knew it would be hers someday.

"Maybe it is too dark to see," Mama said. She opened up the sewing basket and put the dress, needle, and thread back inside. "Could it be that the days are beginning to be shorter already?"

"Emma and I saw caterpillars on her papa's grapevines," Elisa said. "She said that was a sure sign fall was on the way."

Mama rested her head on the back of the rocking chair and closed her eyes. It was one thing to keep everyone happy and fed in the balmy summer weather. How would she manage a cold winter with Papa not well enough to help? As always, she trusted the Lord would provide.

"That reminds me," Emmanuel said. "I have to get up early to harvest the corn. I'm turning in."

Elisa knew how much work and time Emmanuel was putting into the farm. Most mornings, he was already in the fields when the girls came down to breakfast. She was proud of her brother, but she missed the fun they used to have together.

Like the other farms in the area, this one had been planted with wheat and alfalfa to sell for income and with vegetables to provide food for the family over the winter months. Adele and Albertine loved to play hide and seek in the rows of corn, which soon grew taller than they were. There was also a plot of green beans, and rows of carrots, radishes, and potatoes. Strawberries and raspberries grew where the girls could pick them easily, and what didn't get popped in their mouths went into a silver bucket to be taken to Mama.

While Emmanuel was learning to harvest what the

previous owners of the farm had planted, Mama was learning all about canning. It was her goal to line the shelves in the cool basement with neatly packed jars all in rows just as the other farm wives did.

The next morning when Elisa came into the kitchen she saw Emmanuel and Mama looking at corn in a bushel basket. She knew her brother well enough to know he was holding back tears as they talked.

"I'm sorry, Mama," he said. "I checked the corn the first part of the week and I didn't think it was ready to be picked. But look at it now. It's gone coarse. I think it's ruined."

"Some ears look better than others," Mama said as she picked up one ear after another and stripped back the silky husks. "I don't want you to be upset, Em. We'll sort through all the bushels and find some I can put up for us to eat. We can still take a good part of this corn to the mill to be ground into cornmeal, and the rest we may be able to sell to someone to feed to their livestock over the winter."

"What will Papa say, Mama?" Emmanuel asked. "I promised him I would try to get everything harvested on time."

"And he's so proud of all you've done," Mama said. "We're both learning, Em. I had to throw out that whole batch of green beans you brought in for me to put up yesterday. After I had them all sealed in the jars, I realized I had accidentally tossed in the ends I had snapped off the beans! Don't worry, the Lord will honor our efforts and forgive our mistakes, and so will Papa. Rest assured, the Lord will provide."

"I'll help you sort through the corn," Elisa said from the doorway. "At least that way I'll have some time with my favorite brother."

"You mean your only brother, don't you?" Emmanuel said, and Elisa saw the smile she had been missing ever since he had taken on so much family responsibility.

Chapter Seven

The warm days of September did grow shorter, and because the nights grew cooler the leaves on the maple trees became edged in orange and red. But school didn't start until the end of the month in order to allow the children time to help with the harvest, so it still seemed like summer to the Bolli children.

As Emmanuel became more comfortable in his role as caretaker of the farm, he began to teach Elisa and Cecile to feed the pigs and the chickens, gather the eggs, and weed the gardens. They even helped harvest the beans and potatoes.

Cecile preferred to spend her time helping Mama with the sewing, baking, and cooking, so she did her chores as quickly as possible and went back in the house.

Elisa, on the other hand, loved to stay outdoors for hours on end. When her chores were done, she would hike on winding paths through the woods to Third Creek and watch the water striders skim across the water. She always took a bucket or basket along on her walks and came home with blackberries or wild strawberries for Mama to bake in a pie.

Elisa enjoyed spending the summer days with her brother and sisters, but she longed for other friends too. She loved it when the Buffats would stop by on Sunday afternoons with their six children.

Whenever Emmanuel had to walk to the Esperandieus to borrow or return a tool, Elisa was ready to go along at a moment's notice. The five Esperandieu children who had given the Bolli children their first English lessons continued to be a source of joy for Elisa. Mary was exactly Elisa's age, but Elisa preferred to spend time with Mary's older sister, Lily, because Lily had a pony. She gave Elisa riding lessons and taught her how to comb the pony's mane and tail and brush its coat.

Uncle and Aunt Esperandieu were always so kind to the Bolli children, and asked about Papa whenever Elisa visited. The name Esperandieu means "hope in God" in French. The whole family clearly put all their hope and trust in the Lord, and it showed in their kindness to others.

A walk to the Chavannes farm, where Sunday services were held, took even longer because it was beyond the Esperandieu farm. Often the Bollis would walk as far as the Esperandieus, and be offered a ride in a wagon or on horse-back the rest of the way. When it was too rainy or muddy, the Bollis didn't go to services at all.

Services at a meeting of the Open Brethren could last for hours. A typical service began with the singing of a hymn, followed by a prayer, then another hymn and another prayer. One of the elders read a chapter from the Bible, then taught on that chapter. Those in attendance could make comments or expound upon what was read and taught. Often the Lord's Supper was observed. The service closed with a final hymn and prayer.

Going to services gave Elisa a chance to be with her favorite cousin, Emma, and to get to know her other cousins better—especially on days when everyone brought a basket dinner to eat together on the grounds around the Chavannes home.

Still, Elisa wished she could visit her friends Mary and Lily Esperandieu or Emma Chavannes for several days at a time. It was the custom to pack up a day's worth of sewing, a few loaves of bread and a pie, and go visit friends or relatives for a day or so. But with Papa so sick, Mama wasn't doing that kind of visiting, and Elisa was still too young to go alone.

One Sunday after services at the Chavannes farm, Mama announced that the Chavannes had offered to loan Emmanuel their wagon to take her and the children home so she could get back more quickly to check on Papa. Since Emmanuel would be bringing the wagon back the next day, Elisa was invited to stay for the night. Then she and Emmanuel would walk home together.

"Please stay, Elisa!" Emma Chavannes said.

The begging wasn't necessary. Elisa couldn't think of anything she would rather do.

That afternoon, Elisa and Emma spent hours swinging from the wooden swing hanging in the big oak tree in Emma's front yard.

"How do you feel about moving to Tennessee, Elisa?" Emma asked as she gave Elisa another push on the swing. "You never talk about your home in Brazil. Are you ever homesick for it?"

"I miss Josepha and Maria. They were the servants who cared for us," Elisa said. "And I miss going to the marketplace and down by the wharf with Papa. I wish I could take you there and show you all the fish, Emma. They were much larger than the trout in Third Creek."

"I bet you had a lot of fun with your Papa when he was well, didn't you?" Emma asked later when she and Elisa switched places and she climbed into the swing. "Does it make you sad to think of those times? Is that why you never talk about your life there?"

"It does make me sad," Elisa said, giving Emma a push to get her started. "But I'm praying Papa will be well again. Then you will get to know him and see what a wonderful father he is. Besides, I don't talk about Brazil because Mama says we have to think of Tennessee as our home now. I guess we've all been too busy learning English and learning about farm life to be homesick for Brazil."

"Well, I'm sure glad you moved here, Elisa," Emma said. "Come on, let's go pick some berries for supper."

The girls picked red and white currants from a row along

one side of the yard. When the late afternoon rain rolled in, Emma took Elisa inside and taught her some new songs on the piano, including all the stanzas to "The Old Oaken Bucket."

Elisa got to wear one of Emma's nightdresses that night and sleep with her under her big feather comforter. When it was time to leave the next afternoon, Emma picked a huge bunch of flowers from the garden for Elisa to take with her— so many that Emmanuel had to help carry them all!

*   *   *

What fun Elisa had putting vases and jars of the different kinds of flowers all over the house when she got home. She put three bouquets in Papa's room to cheer him. The flowers cheered Elisa for days too. Their sunny faces reminded her of her cousin and best friend, Emma.

"Did you see Albert while you were visiting Emma?" Cecile asked as she and Elisa were drying the dishes that night.

"Why do you ask?" Elisa teased. She knew Cecile was sweet on Albert Chavannes and couldn't resist having a little bit of fun with her older sister.

"Yes, he was there. He asked about you and I told him you were sick with a case of the uglies."

"You are so mean, Elisa!" Cecile said. She snapped the dish-towel in her sister's direction. "Did he really ask about me?"

"Finish drying the dishes by yourself and I'll tell you," Elisa said, and she skipped out onto the front porch leaving Cecile with a stack of dishes to dry.

"You aren't being charitable to me, Lizzie," Cecile said when she plopped down in a rocking chair on the front porch next to her sister a few minutes later.

"You're right, Cile. I apologize. The truth is, I only saw Albert for a few minutes, but he did ask about you. I told him you were busy helping Mama."

"Thanks, Lizzie."

The girls sat silently rocking for a while. They could hear

Mama inside the house telling Albertine and Adele to get into their nightclothes.

"Do you think Albert is handsome?" Cecile asked.

"Well, he is Emma's older brother," Elisa said, "and you know I think Emma's beautiful. I guess that makes Albert handsome, doesn't it?"

The two girls laughed and stared up into the darkening sky together.

"It's hard to imagine that's the same moon we saw from the veranda in Brazil, isn't it?" Cecile said when the light of the full moon broke through the limbs of the maple tree.

"It sure is," Elisa said. "I guess it followed us all the way here."

"When I see the moon it reminds me that God's in His heaven," Cecile said. "As long as I can see the moon, I know everything's going to be all right."

Elisa thought about what her sister said and tried to believe it. She prayed everything would be all right. But Papa slept almost all the time now. Even the younger children were beginning to wonder if he would ever be well.

"Cile," Elisa began after a while. "Mama always says all things work together for good to those who love the Lord, right?"

"Yes, Elisa. That's a verse in Romans. Remember? Reverend Chavannes taught on that passage last week."

"I remember, but I can't help but wonder how Papa's being sick, maybe even dying, is part of the Lord's plan for our good."

"I don't know, Elisa," Cecile said. She reached over to put her hand on top of her sister's. "I just don't know."

* * *

The next Sunday Papa was feeling so poorly that Mama decided to keep the whole family home from services. But Sunday afternoon was visiting day amongst the relatives. The Bolli girls dressed in their Sunday clothes in hopes that someone would come calling and they would see some of their cousins and friends after all.

They didn't have to wait long. Just as the last of the lunch dishes were cleared away, there was a knock at the front door. It was Mr. and Mrs. Buffat and their children: Alfred, thirteen, Gustave, eleven, Marie, eight, Elisa, six, Anna, four, and Emile, two.

"Come in! Come in!" Mama said when she greeted them at the front door. "I'm afraid we don't have furniture in the parlor yet, but I've made some fresh lemonade. Why don't we visit on the back porch."

"That would be just fine, Elise. Especially for this visit," Mr. Buffat said.

The children raced on ahead, through the kitchen, and out the back door. Since they had visited before, they knew just where to go.

A couple of them noticed Elisa at the kitchen table practicing her handwriting and said hello to her on their way through. School would be starting soon, and Elisa wanted to be ready.

"Hello, dear," Mrs. Buffat said when she came into the room. Mama taught the children to stand up in the presence of adults, so Elisa put down her pen and stood. As she did, she noticed Mr. Buffat coming through the kitchen with a burlap bag. Something in the bag was squirming.

"Hello, Mrs. Buffat. What does Mr. Buffat have in his bag?" Elisa asked.

"Come outside and see!" Mrs. Buffat said with a grin.

"Albertine! Adele! Come down to the backyard," Mama yelled up to the younger girls' bedroom window. "There's a surprise here for you!"

Emmanuel and Cecile heard Mama calling too. Soon all the children were gathered on the back porch around Mr. Buffat's squirming burlap bag. Something inside really wanted out!

"What's in there?" Adele asked.

"Why don't I just show you," Mr. Buffat said. He let go of the top of the sack and out came an adorable black and white puppy with shaggy hair, black eyes, and a tail that curled up over his back. The puppy immediately jumped up on Adele and began licking her face.

"A puppy!" she squealed. "It's a puppy!"

"It's your puppy, honey," Mr. Buffat said. "We were at the Chavannes farm for services today, and your Uncle Theodore and Aunt Cecile asked if we would deliver it to you."

"Oh, Mama!" Albertine said. "Is it really ours? I didn't know Papa said yes."

"He said yes," Mama said. The puppy ran to give Mama a lick too.

"He wanted it to be a surprise," Emmanuel said as he turned the puppy over and rubbed it on its tummy. "He told me to let Uncle Theodore know we wanted one of the litter when I was there last week. Thanks for the special delivery, Mr. Buffat."

"We were happy to do it," Mr. Buffat said.

The Buffats stayed most of the afternoon. Mr. and Mrs. Buffat had a short visit with Papa, who also got a visit from the puppy. Adele carried the dog in and put it on the bed, where it ran around in circles on the bedcovers and licked Papa in the face.

"The dog has to stay outside after today, Adele," Papa said. "What are you going to name him?"

"Let's name him Turk!" Adele said.

Everyone was a bit surprised by her choice, but Turk it was.

The rest of the afternoon was spent in the backyard with the younger children chasing the puppy and the puppy chasing them in turn. Soon Turk was so tired he fell fast asleep under the porch steps and Mama told the children to let him be for the rest of the day. Adele had to content herself with lying in the dirt on her stomach and peeking in at the sleeping puppy.

When the excitement was over, Elisa went back to her writing in the kitchen. Alfred Buffat came in to see what she was doing.

"I missed seeing you at services today," Alfred said. He took the chair opposite Elisa's.

"Mama said it was too far for us to be away from Papa," Elisa explained without looking up from her work. She liked Alfred all right, but he was two years older than she, and she was bashful about talking to him.

"There's a Sunday School meeting at our house next week," Alfred said. "Maybe you could come to that. It's a lot closer than the Chavannes farm."

"Maybe," Elisa said. She ventured a quick smile in Alfred's direction.

"What are you working on?" he asked.

"I'm practicing my handwriting by making a list of French words and their English meanings," Elisa said.

"Will you be coming to Spring Place School when it starts up again next week?" Alfred asked.

"Yes. Mama says we'll all go this year except Adele," Elisa said.

"Well that's going to make the room a bit more crowded," Alfred teased.

Spring Place School was a log schoolhouse built on the east corner of the Buffat farm. It had one long room, eighteen feet by twenty-four feet, with a door in the center of the south side and a window on each side of the door. Students sat on long wooden benches. Along one wall was a slanted board used as a table for writing exercises, with a long bench in front of it. Everyone went to school in that one room.

"You'll do fine, Elisa. We have lessons in French and English," Alfred said.

"Are there books for us to use?" Elisa asked. She was getting over her shyness now that she realized Alfred could answer some of the many questions she had about what her new American school would be like.

"We use Webster's Speller," Alfred said. "Intermediate readers read from the New Testament, and advanced readers read from the Old Testament. You can bring this Bible of yours if you want," Alfred said when he noticed Elisa's Bible next to her work on the kitchen table.

"What about arithmetic?" Elisa asked. "Do they have arithmetic books?"

"We have a grammar text, a geography text, and an arithmetic text," Alfred explained, "but not too many of each one. If you have any books of your own, you can bring those along. The teacher has goose quills for everyone."

Just then Mr. and Mrs. Buffat, accompanied by all the little Buffats, came into the kitchen through the back door and announced it was time to go home. Elisa said good-bye to Alfred. She wanted to thank him for making her feel better about school, but she wasn't sure what to say so she didn't say anything. Then he was gone.

Chapter Eight

The first day of school, on the last Monday in September, turned out to be as warm as any day in summer. Still, Cecile, Elisa, and Albertine had insisted on wearing the navy blue wool cloaks their mother had made for them—with the navy bonnets to match. The cloaks weren't too hot to wear in the cool morning mist, but they were bulky and heavy to carry home in the afternoon heat.

"You wanted to wear them, you carry them," Emmanuel said as he set off down the dusty road leaving the girls to trudge home together. The bonnets they had tossed off their heads looked like papooses on their backs.

"Do you like our teacher?" Elisa asked Cecile as the girls finally turned into the lane leading to their farmhouse.

"I think she's just strict enough," Cecile said.

"Alfred said his father was a teacher in Switzerland. He was very strict."

"Do you plan to spend every recess talking to Alfred Buffat?" Cecile teased.

"I might as well since you'll be talking to Albert Chavannes," her sister replied.

"Alfred and Albert," Albertine sang as she skipped up the lane to meet Turk, who was running to greet her. "Alfred and Albert."

"They sound like they should be related to you, Albertine!" Elisa shouted after her little sister.

*   *   *

As the school year continued, Elisa became absorbed in her studies and was soon doing all her lessons in English. She loved telling the other children about Brazil when they had a geography lesson on South America. But most of all she loved being able to see her friends and cousins Mary and Lily Esperandieu and Emma Chavannes every day instead of just on Sundays.

The warm days of Indian summer were the most beautiful days Elisa had spent in the new country. She did her chores quickly after school so she could go on her hiking adventures and be home before dark. The leaves on the trees turned completely red, orange and gold, then fell to create a multi-colored carpet for Turk to run through. Elisa loved hearing the leaves crunch under her high-button shoes. Now when she looked up she could see blue sky through the branches of the trees.

Instead of summer berries, Elisa collected walnuts and chestnuts on her walks. "You're gathering nuts for winter just like the squirrels," Mama teased. Some days Elisa took her accordion into the woods with her and played and sang from her favorite rock on the creek bank. She thought the sound was enchanting, but Turk howled at the high notes.

One Friday, Elisa invited Emma to come home to spend the weekend. Emma loved to hike too, and she and Elisa started out early the next day and climbed all the way up through the woods to a rolling green ridge. From there they could see the Smoky Mountains in the blue haze forty miles away.

The girls picked the last of the high meadow wildflowers to put on their straw hats. "Elisa, promise me we'll travel to the moutains together someday," Emma said as the girls were leaving.

"I promise!" Elisa said. "We'll go in a finely polished black buggy pulled by two matching black horses."

"Oh, yes! How perfect," Emma said as the girls ran down the trail.

*   *   *

As time went by Turk turned from a fluffy ball into a long-legged dog, but he still had the exuberance of a puppy. Adele and Albertine kept their promise to feed and water him, but the whole family became involved in his training. Keeping him in the yard was a particular challenge.

Elisa was surprised one afternoon after school when she saw Turk coming out of her father's bedroom.

"I thought Papa didn't want Turk in the house," Elisa said.

"He finds him good company when Adele and I are busy in the kitchen," Mama said with a wink. "Guess you could say he changed his mind."

Not only was the dog in the house, he was taking his afternoon naps on the bed with Papa. He curled up wherever a ray of sunlight beamed across the coverlet. Some days Papa would reach out and pat Turk on the head. But more and more often, he was asleep himself and didn't even know Turk was there.

The distraction of school and of enjoying the last warm days of autumn outside kept the children from focusing on their father's failing health. They would all visit him to tell him what they had learned each day. They always went in to kiss him goodnight before going to bed. But it wasn't until the colder days of November kept them inside more that they realized how violent his coughing spells had become and how much he slept.

Dr. Clark rode out from Knoxville regularly to see Papa, but nothing he suggested that Mama do for Papa seemed to help very much.

"We learned all about Thanksgiving at school today!" Albertine said when the children burst into the house after school one day. Then they all told Mama, Papa, and Adele about the Pilgrims and Plymouth Rock, and how the Indians taught the English how to grow corn. They told them how the Pilgrims held a feast to express their gratitude for their new home in America.

"We have a lot to be thankful for too," Mama said. "Since this will be our first Thanksgiving ever, I think we should celebrate with a big Thanksgiving dinner in our new home. Don't you think so, dear?" Mama asked Papa. Papa smiled and nodded his approval, and the children were delighted.

Preparations began the weekend before the big day. Mama asked Emmanuel to take the door off the log shed out back and scrub it good. She also asked him to empty two rain barrels and let them dry. The girls couldn't imagine what all this had to do with Thanksgiving until they came into the dining room to see Mama and Emmanuel putting the door on top of the two barrels to create a long, sturdy, dining room table.

"Now, I'm going up in the attic to find some table linens," Mama said. "While I'm up there, I'm going to have another look for my wedding veil. I haven't thought about it in months."

The girls busied themselves in the kitchen pitting cherries and peeling apples for the pies. A big kettle of cider was boiling so Mama could make apple butter, and the whole kitchen smelled wonderful.

Aunt Cecile and Uncle Theodore and their children, Laure, fourteen, and Henri, almost six, were coming for dinner too, so there was a lot of cooking to do.

Elisa put down her knife and dried her hands when she saw Mama come into the kitchen with an armful of white linen and lace.

"Did you find the veil, Mama?" she asked. "Let me see!"

"No, honey, I didn't, but I still don't think we should give up hope. You must have packed it in a trunk other than the one with the linens. We'll come across it someday.

"Meanwhile, we have our work cut out for us. These linens are turning yellow already. Wouldn't Josepha and Maria have a fit if they could see them? We have to boil them in hot water and get them out in the sun early enough in the day to bleach them out again. The sun isn't nearly hot enough this time of year to bleach them properly, but we must try. Hurry, now!"

By late afternoon the linens were ready. They weren't pure white, but they had dried in the late autumn sun. Soon they were in place on the makeshift dining-room table. No one cloth was large enough, so Mama and the girls layered them, alternating linen and lace until they created a table Mama dubbed "fit for the angels."

Cecile folded linen napkins into swan shapes and positioned one at each place. From the trunk in the bedroom, Mama brought out her best silver flatware and two candelabra that she hadn't used since they left Pernambuco. Emmanuel polished all the silver until it gleamed, and then the girls set the table.

"Aren't you going to bed, Mama?" Elisa asked when she noticed her mother had taken her coffee and a kitchen chair into the dining room and was sitting and staring at the beautifully set table. Elisa had forgotten about the elegant dinners her mother and father had hosted in Brazil. Now she was reminded of just how much her mother had given up to come to America.

"I suppose it's time," Mama said. "Here. Help me cover the table with this piece of muslin I cut off the bolt. Our masterpiece will be unveiled on Thursday, just before the guests arrive."

For weeks the French-Swiss women had been trading recipes at Sunday services, so Mama knew exactly what the menu for Thanksgiving would be. On Wednesday, Emmanuel came back from hunting with Uncle Theodore with a fresh turkey that he and Mama plucked and cleaned. The turkey was stuffed with cornbread dressing and roasted on a spit over the fireplace.

In addition to the cherry and apple pies, there was mincemeat pie and pumpkin pie, and three loaves of homemade bread ready to go. The children couldn't wait to taste the corn pudding and cranberry sauce Mama made. She also made a cream sauce for the last of the fresh garden peas that had been stored in the basement since before the first frost.

Aunt Cecile and Uncle Theodore operated a candle-making business in one of the buildings on their farm, so they brought beautiful wine-colored candles for Mama's candelabra. Finally the candles were lit, the food was on the table, and everyone gathered in the dining room.

"Where are Emmanuel and Uncle Theodore?" Adele asked.

"They'll be here soon," Mama said.

Just then the two of them entered the room. They had locked arms to make a chair for Papa, and they carried him right to his place at the head of the table.

Elisa saw the tears in her mother's eyes glistening in the candlelight.

"Papa! You're back at the table with us!" Albertine said.

"Yes, darling girl, I am," Papa said. "Shall we bow and thank the Lord for this wonderful bounty?"

It was so good to have Papa praying at the table again that the children didn't mind if the turkey and corn pudding got cold while they waited for the amens.

Elisa peeked at her father through one of the candelabra during the grace. Uncle Theodore had helped him dress in his best gray suit, but Elisa thought it looked far too big for him now. The starched, white shirt collar stuck out all around Papa's neck instead of fitting snuggly. This made his tie seem far too bulky. It hadn't been nearly so obvious that her father had lost weight when he was in bed under the covers.

Uncle Theodore carved the turkey and gave the drumsticks to Adele and Henri because they were the youngest. Papa took just a few bites of his food before asking to be excused to go lie down.

"Let me help," Mama said, and she laid down her napkin and stood up.

"We'll take care of him, Elise," Uncle Theodore said as he and Emmanuel picked Papa up again. "You stay here and enjoy this delicious feast you've prepared."

An awkward silence fell over the room after they carried Papa out.

"I think I'll move around here to give us all a bit more room," Emmanuel said when he returned, and he slipped into the chair Papa had vacated. It was easier to get back into the holiday spirit without the empty place at the end of the table. Soon Papa was napping with Turk, and everyone else was passing their plates for thirds and fourths.

* * *

The month between Thanksgiving and Christmas seemed to fly by. Each day after school the children would rush in to see if anything had come by post and been delivered by one of the neighbors who had gone in to Knoxville for supplies.

One day there was a box from Josepha and Maria in Brazil. Inside were two loaves of holiday bread traditionally enjoyed at Christmas in Pernambuco. Because of the European influence in Brazil, residents along the coast were accustomed to enjoying both Italian *panettone* and German *stollen*. Scattered around the carefully wrapped loaves were handfuls of the wonderful *bolas quemada*, balls of caramel candy the children remembered fondly.

"How sweet of Josepha and Maria to try to keep us from being homesick for Christmas in Brazil," Mama said.

Then, just a week before Christmas, on the last day of school before the holidays, Adele greeted the children at the door.

"Grandfather Bolli's box is here! It's here from Paris!" Adele announced. Mr. Buffat had dropped it off at the house on his way back from town that day.

The children stood in the front foyer staring down at the big box covered with stamps as if it had fallen out of the sky from another planet.

"We won't be opening that until Christmas Eve," Mama called to them. "You might as well stop staring at it and come help me bake the bricelets."

Mama always made Swiss bricelets for Christmas. They were lacy, wafer-like cookies baked in bricelet irons over an open fire. At Christmas time, fresh bricelets sprinkled with sugar were put into baskets lined with white linen to give to the neighbors. Ginger cakes and pies were also given as gifts, as were preserves and jellies.

The next week went by very fast as the children helped with the baking and decorating. Cecile and Elisa made brightly colored paper flowers to put on the spruce tree Emmanuel had set up in the front parlor. The extra ones they affixed to the curtain rod in Papa's room. On the branches they put balls of cotton to simulate snow just as they had done in Brazil. It was much colder in Tennessee in December than in Brazil, but it still hadn't snowed. The cotton made it seem more Christmasy.

Under the tree the children arranged the figures of the *presepio*—the Brazilian nativity scene. A second *crèche* with figures hand-carved of Brazilwood was on the mantel.

"How will we celebrate Christmas this year, Mama?" Elisa asked as she sat at the kitchen table looking through a stack of postcards bearing Christmas greetings. Reading the messages from friends and relatives in Switzerland and Brazil, Elisa noticed how many people had inquired about Papa.

"Much as we did in Brazil, Elisa," Mama said. "Here little children talk about Santa Claus instead of *Papa Noel*, but the real meaning of Christmas is the same everywhere for those who celebrate the birth of our Lord.

"With Papa so sick, I don't think we'll be doing any entertaining here. But the Chavannes family is having a party after services on Christmas Eve, and I've arranged for you to go with the Esperandieus. When you get home we'll open our gifts here together."

Elisa was excited about a party, and about seeing herself and her friends all dressed up for the holiday, but she was sad to think of going to services without Mama and Papa. Still,

Christmas Eve went just as Mama planned, ending with everyone except Papa gathered around the tree in the parlor.

As always, the box from Grandfather Bolli was the highlight as the children tore through the tissue paper to find the gifts and chocolate. "Slow down, children!" Mama shouted above the excitement. "Open your gifts one at a time so we can all see what you received."

Emmanuel already had found his gift in the box, so he got to open his first.

"Oh, look! It's a brass telescope!" he exclaimed.

"Now we'll really be able to see the moon when we sit out on the porch on summer evenings," Elisa said.

"You're assuming I let you look through it," Emmanuel laughed as he tossed a ball of wrapping paper at Elisa.

"Let's open our gifts together, Cile," Elisa suggested. "They are exactly the same size so they are probably just alike. If you open yours first, I won't be surprised."

"Good idea, Elisa. One, two, three, go!"

When the girls tore away the red velvet ribbons and red and green paper holding their packages together, out fell exquisite lace collars and cuffs. Grandfather Bolli wanted his Tennessee granddaughters to look just as fine as Parisian girls when they went to fancy parties. He had spared no expense in choosing the lace.

"These are so beautiful," Elisa said. "I wonder if we'll ever be invited to a party that's fancy enough for us to wear them."

"We'll just have to have one!" Cecile said.

"May we open our presents now?" Adele called out. "May we, please?"

Everyone laughed when they looked at Adele and Albertine and saw that they had been sitting patiently with two gifts on each of their laps. Since Christmas was special for younger children, and Grandfather Bolli still thought of Albertine as younger than she really was, he was doubly generous with both of them.

"You've been so patient," Mama said. "Open at once."

Albertine opened her larger present first. It was a beautiful waxhead doll with eyes that opened and shut. A separate box contained a tiny porcelain tea set.

"Hurry and open yours, Adele," Bertie said. "See if you got a doll too."

"I did! I did!" Adele shouted as she reached through the packing to retrieve a raven-haired doll with blue eyes. "She can come to your tea party!" In a separate box, Adele found a parrot carved from Brazilwood.

"Oh, look! He looks just like Columbo, the parrot we had on our ship!" Adele said.

The children had a merry time looking at all their gifts, and stayed up much later than usual before going up to bed.

* * *

Christmas morning they were up early to fix breakfast. It was the custom in Brazil for children to serve their parents breakfast in bed before they could look around the house for more little hidden gifts.

Emmanuel stoked the fire, collected the eggs, and made a pot of hot coffee. Cecile scrambled eggs with cheese and cooked them and some *saucisson*, homemade Swiss sausage, in a big iron skillet. The other girls made fresh biscuits. Elisa put some peach preserves in a crystal bowl on the tray and Cecile added a sprig of holly.

Emmanuel declared the tray ready to go and the five of them went down the hall together. "*Boas Festas*! Merry Christmas! *Joyeux Noel*!" the children called out as they knocked on the door.

But what they saw when they entered the bedroom surprised them. Mama was sitting in a straight-back chair right next to Papa's bed still in the green velvet dress she had worn on Christmas Eve. She turned to look at the children, and they knew immediately that she had been awake all night.

"Shhhh!" Mama said as she motioned for the children to

be quiet. "He had a bad night," she whispered. "Oh, how lovely," she said when she saw the tray. "Please take it back to the kitchen. I'll join you there shortly."

The children sat quietly around the kitchen table staring at the untouched tray of food. This was their first Christmas in America, but there would be no joy in the new year without Papa.

Chapter Nine

The next few days passed slowly and solemnly. Papa did not improve. He developed a high fever and needed someone with him around the clock to fan him and put cold compresses on his head.

Dr. Clark made two special trips from Knoxville in his buggy to see Papa, but he didn't have any medicine that would help bring down the fever. He determined that even bleeding Papa with leeches would do nothing to clear up his lungs, which had become more congested because he was too weak to get out of bed. Elisa heard the word "pneumonia" used when Mama and the doctor were talking in hushed tones in the foyer.

The children spent the holiday season playing with the toys and books they received for Christmas, but without their usual holiday joy. Everyone had to tiptoe through the house so Papa could rest as much as possible. When Mama sat down in her rocking chair by the fire in the kitchen during the day, she was soon fast asleep. Finally, Emmanuel, Cecile, and Elisa convinced her they could take turns caring for Papa at night so she could get some rest.

New Year's Eve arrived and Elisa was with Papa when the stroke of midnight signaled the beginning of 1854. She had just placed a fresh compress on his head when Cecile came in to relieve her.

"Happy New Year, Sister," Cecile whispered as she put her arm around Elisa's shoulders. The light from the candle on the bedside table cast the girls' shadows on the wall next to Papa's bed.

"I wish I thought it would be happy," Elisa whispered back as she looked down at Papa, who lay very still with his eyes closed. "What's that noise outside?"

"The neighbors are shooting their guns in the air to celebrate the New Year," Cecile said. She walked to the window and looked in the direction of town. "We may even be hearing the fireworks they're shooting from the riverbank in Knoxville."

"Remember going to the beach on New Year's Eve in Pernambuco?" Elisa asked Cecile when her sister returned to Papa's bedside.

In all the coastal cities of Brazil on New Year's Eve the residents, dressed all in white, gathered on the beaches to watch the fireworks. It was a joyous time of celebration.

"Papa was so handsome in his white suit," Cecile said. "That seems like a very long time ago instead of just last year, doesn't it?"

Elisa left Cecile with Papa and went up to bed. Before blowing out the candle, she wrote in her journal: "I don't like to see 1854 written out in numerals. I'm too fearful of seeing it engraved on my father's tombstone."

Reverend and Mrs. Chavannes, Aunt Cecile and Uncle Theodore, often came by to pray with the Bollis as did the Esperandieus and the Buffats. They prayed for Papa to be miraculously healed, but that if it was not the Lord's will, that he be taken quickly to heaven. When they came they brought baskets of food and jars of homemade soup so Mama wouldn't have to cook. Elisa was always glad to see her friends when they came with their parents, but she wished they could be as happy together as they had been in the summer and autumn.

In addition to Papa's sad condition, the weather was ugly. One light snow the first week of January brightened up the landscape for a day or two, so the children bundled up to play in it. Turk raced around trying to bite the snowflakes and the children laughed together for the first time since Christmas Eve.

After that snowfall, however, the days turned gray and dreary. By the middle of January a cold winter rain had settled in. One night Elisa sat by Papa's bed listening to the rain pelting against the window. The candle was lit on the table by the bed. Elisa had just returned to the bedroom with a fresh basin of water from the kitchen. She took the compress off Papa's head and dipped it in the cool water. Then she wrung it out and placed it back across his forehead.

Just then Papa opened his eyes and looked right up into Elisa's face.

"Are you an angel?" he asked. And he smiled a wonderful Papa smile.

"No, Papa," Elisa said. "It's me, Elisa. I'm just changing your compress to keep you cooler."

"Oh, Elisa, yes. My precious daughter. I love you, Elisa."

"I love you, too, Papa," Elisa said. His eyes closed again before he saw her tears.

* * *

After that night, Elisa never saw Papa's blue eyes open again. Cecile and Emmanuel had similar brief moments with their father; times Mama called the Lord's gift to each of them. Mama took Albertine and Adele in to say good-bye to Papa too. And Turk, well, Turk never left Papa's bed. Emmanuel had to carry him to the back door and force him to go out in the rain to relieve himself.

On the morning of January 26, 1854, Elisa awoke before daylight to strange sounds in the house. She could hear men's voices in the foyer mingled with the sound of the men stamping their boots on the mat to clean off the mud from outdoors. Still in her nightclothes, she peeked down the stairs into the foyer. There she saw Dr. Clark and Reverend Chavannes talking to Mama and Emmanuel.

Elisa slipped back under her covers without waking Cecile. She wondered why Emmanuel hadn't wakened her to take her turn caring for Papa, yet something told her she didn't really want to know.

Soon Mama came into her room.

"Elisa. Cecile. Wake up and come into the little girls' room. There's something I have to tell you, and I want you all to be together."

Albertine and Adele rubbed the sleep from their eyes and leaned against each side of Mama, who was sitting on the edge of Adele's bed. Cecile and Elisa sat on the edge of Albertine's bed, her feather comforter wrapped around their shoulders.

"You know Papa has been very ill," Mama began. "Last night, when Emmanuel was with him, Papa started talking to the angels," Mama said. "Emmanuel said Papa sat straight up. That's when he ran to wake me."

"Then what happened, Mama?" Adele asked.

"As soon as we got back to the bedroom, Papa laid down again. I took his hand in both of mine and told him I loved him. He looked at me so peacefully, girls, so peacefully," Mama said, and the tears began to flow down her cheeks. "Then he went to be with the Lord."

"Papa's gone?" Albertine asked.

"Yes, sweetheart. He's gone to heaven," Mama said.

Elisa didn't know if she could move. She didn't even know if she would ever be able to breathe again. But after a few moments she and Cecile joined Mama and the little girls on Adele's bed. The five of them hugged and cried together as Mama tried to hold and rock them all at once.

Soon the room began to fill with a grayish light. Elisa realized it was morning, but she couldn't imagine why. How could another day dawn when Papa was dead? There should have been so many more days with Papa. He was only forty-nine years old when he died.

*   *   *

People began stopping by almost as soon as the children

were dressed and gathered in the kitchen. Emmanuel built a big fire in the fireplace and started the coffee brewing before going to lie down for a bit. He had been up all night. After Papa died, he had walked to the Esperandieus and borrowed a horse to ride for Dr. Clark and Reverend Chavannes. Once they had all arrived back at the house, the doctor had declared Papa dead. Reverend Chavannes had prayed with Mama and talked to her about Papa's funeral.

Soon Uncle and Aunt Esperandieu arrived. Mr. Esperandieu and the other men carried a large black coffin into the house and set it in the middle of the parlor. Aunt Esperandieu helped Mama bathe Papa and dress him in his best gray suit, with the same shirt and tie he had worn at Thanksgiving. Then the men carried Papa's body into the parlor and laid it in the coffin. Mama combed his blonde hair to one side and placed his hands one on top of another. In his right hand she placed a silver cross. One that used to hang by the front door in Pernambuco.

Cecile and Elisa knew all these preparations were taking place, but they tried to keep Adele and Albertine busy in the kitchen by making breakfast for them. Once Papa was all arranged in his coffin, the adults came back into the kitchen. Emmanuel had come back downstairs and was with them.

"Children," Mama said. "It's time for you to say good-bye to Papa one last time." Together, the family went into the parlor to see Papa lying in his coffin. Elisa wasn't sure she would be able to force her feet to carry her into the room. Cecile took her hand, and together they slowly approached the coffin.

Mama was right. Papa did look peaceful. His eyes were closed now, and the expression on his face looked almost like he was having a pleasant dream. He looked young again. Elisa hadn't realized how the months of illness had left lines on Papa's face until she noticed that they were gone.

"Good-bye, Papa," Elisa said when it was her turn to give him a kiss on the cheek and place her warm hand on his cold ones. "I will love you every day that I live."

After the family said their good-byes, Reverend Chavannes went in to close the coffin. Then the door to the parlor was also closed, leaving Papa all alone, as was the custom in Switzerland.

More neighbors stopped by throughout the day bringing pies, sausages, bread, and an array of cookies and cakes that would have delighted the children under other circumstances. Elisa just looked at the food. The lump in her throat seemed to grow larger as the day wore on. She couldn't imagine how she would swallow anything ever again.

The discussion in the kitchen was all about deaths and funerals. The French-Swiss people who had lived in Tennessee for several years explained to Mama how services and burials were handled differently here than in the old country. Elisa could tell that her mother was trying very hard to understand all that was being said. But she was so very tired.

In Switzerland, before the immigrants left, anyone who died was buried in a plain black coffin like Papa's, and left in a room alone until the funeral. Only the men, dressed completely in black, went to the services or the cemetery for the burial.

Among worldly people, the friends and family would gather later at the home of the deceased for eating and drinking raucously together. The French-Swiss people who were Christians didn't believe in that kind of behavior. That's why they had decided not to socialize after funerals at all. When the neighbors talking to Mama told her of the funerals they had attended in Tennessee, she was surprised to hear visitation was not only allowed after the service, but encouraged. She was also surprised to hear that it was the custom in the new country for relatives to "sit up" with the deceased until the service.

That night, after everyone had returned to their own homes, Mama gathered the children in the kitchen and encouraged them to select at least one thing from the array of donated foods to eat in order to keep up their strength. The children did as they were told and brought their plates to the table.

Mama sat at one end and Emmanuel sat at the other. The children stared at Mama, realizing this was the first time in months she had stayed at the table with them without excusing herself to take a tray to Papa.

"Gracious and merciful Lord," Mama prayed. "We thank You for welcoming our beloved husband and father into Your presence this day. We praise You for sending Your own precious Son to die for us so that we do not have to die, but have eternal life through faith in Him." Mama's shoulders began to shake. She was crying, and couldn't continue praying.

"Fill us with your strength now, Lord," Emmanuel continued. "May all that we do now and in the days to come, our thoughts and our deeds, bring glory to You. In Jesus' name we pray. Amen."

"Thank you, Emmanuel," was all Mama said as she picked up a fork and began poking at the food on her plate. After supper, Mama suddenly seemed to brighten a bit.

"I want you to bring me all the candles and candleholders in the house," Mama said. "Hurry now."

The children scattered and returned with the candles from each of their bedrooms. They put them all, plus Mama's fancy candelabra now kept on the parlor mantel, around the oil lamp on the kitchen table. Mama took one of the long, wooden matches out of the iron matchbox on the wall and began to light the candles one by one.

"Follow me," she said at last. Each child chose a candle or two to carry, and the lighted procession made its way from the kitchen down the hall and into the parlor. Once the candles were set about, the room seemed to glow with a holy presence.

"You children go on to sleep now," Mama said as she

hugged each one in turn. "I'm going to sit up with Papa for a while. There is a time for old customs and a time for new ones. This is a new one I want to observe."

The glow from the parlor into the foyer was more than enough light for the children to see to go upstairs to bed. Elisa took Adele by the hand and Cecile took Albertine by hers. They got the little girls tucked into bed before climbing under their own covers.

To Elisa's surprise, the exhaustion of the day overtook her and she fell to sleep quickly. But she awoke an hour or so later to the sounds of Cecile crying in her bed.

"I love you, Cile," Elisa said in the dark.

"I love you, Lizzie," Cecile said in return.

Then the tears came to Elisa as well. She wasn't sobbing. She was just lying on her back with her eyes open, letting the tears spill down the sides of her face, trickle into her ears, and sop her pillow. There was no end to them, so it seemed hopeless to even try to wipe them away.

Chapter Ten

At the first signs of daylight, Elisa decided she might as well get up and write some of the feelings that had kept her awake most of the night in her journal. She noticed Cecile had finally managed to drop off to sleep, so she moved quietly out of bed and to the desk she and Cecile shared, where she pulled out her journal and a new goose quill pen. A shawl draped around her shoulders took away some of the early morning chill.

At first, Elisa couldn't arrive at any words that made enough sense to write down. She was numb, and couldn't imagine that she would ever have anything to say to anyone again. She bowed her head and tried to pray, but again, no words would come. It was just too soon to give any form to her pain.

Finally she began to think of writing to Papa, of pouring her heart out to him. One line at a time, she wrote a poem in his memory without even intending to do so.

> *Oh! Father dear, come back to me,*
> *My heart is sad, I long for thee.*
> *Could I but hear thy laugh again*
> *'Twould ease my mind from all this pain.*
> *I know with Jesus you abide,*
> *And all the saints are by your side,*
> *Yet it does my heart such good to know*
> *You still see the ones who love you so.*

"What are you writing?" Cecile asked when she awoke

79

and saw Elisa seated at the desk.

"Just some of my thoughts and feelings. Did you sleep well?"

"I did for a while. I wish I could wake up and find out that it was all a bad dream—that Papa's still down in his bed with Mama, and that he's beginning to feel better."

"I know. I found myself thinking that if we just stayed in our room all day, we wouldn't have to face going to Papa's service."

"We can't leave Mama to go through this day alone, Lizzie."

"I know," Elisa said. "Let's get dressed and get Adele and Albertine up and dressed. Then we can all go downstairs together."

When Cecile and Elisa went into the younger girls' bedroom, the girls were just waking up. They were still in that period of forgetfulness that sleep brings. As soon as Albertine remembered what had happened the day before, she began to cry. Then Adele began to cry too.

"We need to be strong for Mama today, girls," Cecile said. "It's right to be sad. The Lord would want us to be sad about losing Papa, and so would Mama. But it's time to face the day, so let's get dressed."

Mama and Emmanuel were sitting at the kitchen table talking when the girls came down. The fire crackling in the kitchen fireplace took the chill out of the room, but not out of the hearts of those Papa had left behind.

"Here are my girls," Mama said. She stood up to hug each one in turn. "Emmanuel and I are talking about the service today. Reverend Chavannes gave us some hymns to consider. He also said it would be appropriate for any of you who wanted to say something about Papa to do so."

"I couldn't say anything, Mama," Albertine sobbed. "If I tried, I would only cry."

"That's all right, dear. I just wanted you to know you could if you wanted to."

Elisa thought about the poem she had written at daylight. It did make her feel better to read it. Maybe it would make the rest of the family feel better too.

"I do have a poem I could read," she said to no one in particular.

"What did you say, dear?" Mama asked. Elisa had spoken so softly, Mama wasn't sure she had heard her correctly.

"I said I have written a poem I could read if you would like."

"I think that would be wonderful, dear. There's a good place for it right after Reverend Chavannes reads some of Papa's favorite Scripture verses. I know that would make Papa very proud," Mama said.

Elisa pulled away from the table and sat on a high stool near the back door. She watched her mother, brother, and sisters without really seeing them. She felt as if she were dreaming. Like this wasn't really happening, and they weren't really planning Papa's funeral service.

But it was happening. Somehow she had to begin to accept Papa's death as Mama seemed to be doing. She didn't understand that working through the details of the things that had to be done was getting them all through the first few days of this horrible grief.

Outside the kitchen window, a pair of cardinals pecked at some seed Mama had put out on a stump, then flew back under the eaves to keep from getting soaked by the rain that was coming down. It had been raining for days, but now the rain seemed to be falling in sheets, like water tossed from giant buckets in heaven.

Don't you know what has happened, birds? Elisa wanted to say. *Papa's dead. You can't just go on looking for food as if it still matters that you eat. Papa is dead. The world can't go on as it was.*

Certainly Elisa knew she couldn't. She would never, ever be the same again.

*   *   *

The funeral service was scheduled to begin at one o'clock. Mama and the children were dressed and ready to go by eleven thirty. Mama wore a black dress and a black hat with a veil that Mrs. Chavannes sent over for her. The girls all had on dark dresses, and Emmanuel had on his only suit, a dark gray one like Papa's. The girls wore their navy blue wool cloaks again. This time, they would need them.

At noon, Reverend and Mrs. Chavannes came to pray with the family and take them to Spring Place Presbyterian Church, the neighborhood church chosen for the service because it was closest to the house and had room for all the French-Swiss to gather. Because of the rain, only two of the Chavannes children, Emma and Albert, came with them. Leon Chavannes stayed at home with the younger children.

Elisa was glad to see Emma when the Chavannes family came into the house, but she didn't know what to say to her friend. It was a relief to realize that nothing had to be said at all. Emma just walked up to Elisa and put her arms around her. It felt good.

Reverend Chavannes was driving the large family buggy, and Albert Chavannes brought the wagon to carry Papa's coffin. The men who were serving as pallbearers arrived in the Esperandieu buggy just as the family was ready to leave. They loaded Papa's coffin onto the wagon. Emmanuel rode with Albert and Papa. Mama and the girls climbed into the buggies wherever there was room, and the small procession started out for the church in the pouring rain.

Aunt Cecile and Uncle Theodore were waiting inside the door of the green frame church when the procession arrived. They ushered Mama and the children into a side room and prayed with them until it was time for the service to begin.

When the family heard the organist play the first few chords of "O God, Our Help in Ages Past," they knew it was time for them to file into the front pew.

Emmanuel led Mama into the pew first, then came Cecile, then Albertine, then Elisa who held Adele's hand.

Elisa tried to sing along with the hymn. She knew her mouth was moving but she wasn't sure if any sounds were coming out. All she could think of as the rain pounded against the church windows was the sunny summer afternoon she had played this same hymn for Papa on her accordion.

"'For we are strangers before thee, and sojourners, as were all our fathers,'" Reverend Chavannes read from 1 Chronicles 29:15. "'Our days on the earth are as a shadow, and there is none abiding.'"

Then he turned to the Psalms. "'As for man, his days are as grass,'" he read from Psalm 103:15-16. "'As a flower of the field, so he flourisheth. For the wind passeth over it, and it is gone; and the place thereof shall know it no more.'"

That isn't true about Papa, Elisa thought as she struggled to take the words of the Scripture into her heart for comfort. *I still know Papa.... I still remember everything about Papa ...even though he is gone from here.*

Elisa was jarred from her thoughts by the realization that Reverend Chavannes was looking directly at her over the top of his glasses, and Adele was squeezing her hand much more tightly than before. Everyone was waiting for her to read her poem.

Letting go of Adele's hand, and picking up her French Bible, Elisa slowly made her way up to the front of the church. Reverend Chavannes pulled a wooden box behind the pulpit, and Elisa climbed up on it so she would be able to see the congregation and they would be able to see her.

It wasn't until Elisa looked out over the rows of people that she realized that so many had ventured out in the rain to pay tribute to her father. He had only lived in America six months when he died, but this group of immigrants was already a strong community of faith. When one family suffered a loss, it was felt by all.

Elisa really didn't need her Bible. She had written her poem out on a separate piece of paper that she tucked in the Bible next to Psalm 23. She just brought the Bible along for comfort. Somehow it made her feel Papa was close to her.

Elisa's knees felt weak and wobbly when she stepped down off the box. She didn't remember reading the words to the poem at all. But walking back to the pew, she realized she must have gotten the words out because everyone in her family was crying. Many of the men and women in the congregation were sniffling or had handkerchiefs up to their noses, too.

After the last hymn, Reverend Chavannes closed the service by reading Psalm 119:50, the verse Papa had chosen to be engraved on his tombstone. "'This is my comfort in my affliction: for thy word hath quickened me.'"

It wasn't the first time Elisa had heard that verse that day. Mama had read it to the children that morning. She had explained to them that the verse was a testament to Papa's faith—that he knew that his life would be preserved for all eternity because of his belief in Jesus.

There was no doubt in Elisa's mind or heart that everything had happened as Papa believed it would, and that he was with Jesus even then. Still, it was so hard to think of his body going to its grave.

After the service, the family gathered at the back of the church to receive hugs and condolences from those who had come to the service. They huddled together as the pallbearers carried Papa's coffin down the center aisle and outside to the wagon that was now waiting to take it to the cemetery at Third Creek.

Still, the rain came down in torrents. "Elise, I see no reason why you and the girls should be out in this soaking rain," Reverend Chavannes said softly to Mama. "Let us get the coffin safely on its way, then I'll take you by the house before going on to the cemetery."

Since in Switzerland only the men went to funerals or cemeteries, the suggestion didn't seem strange to Mama at all. She nodded her agreement that she and the girls should be taken home instead of to the cemetery to stand in the rain by Papa's grave.

Elisa wanted to object. She wasn't ready to part ways with Papa. But she knew her mother needed the support of all her children now. If that was what Mama thought was best, that was what Elisa would do.

By the time Elisa ran from the door of the church to the Chavannes buggy, the bottom half of her skirt was sopping wet. Only the cloaks they wore protected Elisa and her sisters from the bone-chilling cold. The buggy slowly followed behind the wagon with Papa's black coffin on it, but when the house came into view, Reverend Chavannes turned his buggy up the lane to let the women out before proceeding to the gravesite. Elisa turned her head to catch another glimpse of Papa's coffin as it went on down the road. Only Emmanuel went to the cemetery with Papa and the other men.

Chapter Eleven

Elisa and the other girls went upstairs to change out of their wet clothes as soon as they got in the house. Mama went straight to the kitchen to stoke up the fire and put on some coffee.

Even though there wouldn't be the kind of celebration the French-Swiss had found so objectionable amongst those who attended the National Protestant Church in Switzerland, there would be a quiet gathering of the community at the house. Some of the women were already beginning to arrive with more pies and breads.

Looking out their upstairs window, Elisa and Cecile could see the wagon with the coffin going on down the road. They could even see the pallbearers getting the coffin off the wagon. Water poured off the brims of their black stovepipe hats each time they looked down. Then they carried the coffin over a hill to the gravesite, and the girls knew that was the last they would see of their father on this earth.

"I'm going downstairs to see if I can help Mama with anything," Cecile said as she buttoned up her old, but dry pair of high button shoes. "Are you coming?"

"I'll be down in a minute," Elisa said. "I want to go up in the attic and look for Mama's veil again first. I think it would really cheer her up to see it, don't you?"

"I do," Cecile said. "But having us close by is good for her too, so don't be too long." Cecile went to the door, then stopped and turned to look at Elisa again. "By the way," she said. "I loved your poem. It helped me a lot, and I'm proud of you for having the courage to stand up and read it today."

"Thanks, Cile."

Elisa finished changing clothes quickly. She could hear the door opening and closing in the foyer and more voices talking all at once. The smell of wet wool wafted up the stairwell as everyone shed their wet coats and hats and tried to dry off in front of the fire in the parlor.

Really, there were two reasons Elisa felt compelled to go up to the attic. She really did want to find the veil, but she also thought she might have a better view of the cemetery from the tiny attic windows.

Down came the attic ladder and up went Edouard Bolli's second daughter, hoping for just one more look at the coffin that held his dear body. Going up on tiptoes to peer out of the small opening, however, Elisa realized all she could see that she hadn't seen from her window below were more leafless trees wrestling with the wind.

Elisa sat down on the trunk that Cecile, Mama, and she had all thoroughly searched and looked around the attic for any other likely place the veil could be packed. She spotted another trunk across the room and moved toward it with determination.

Pushing open the lid, Elisa saw that the trunk was full of the personal belongings from Papa's office in Pernambuco. There was the wooden nut bowl that had been the focus of her attention while she waited for Papa that last Saturday morning. Wrapped in the banner of the Swiss Embassy that had hung on Papa's wall was the mantel clock. It lay deathly silent in its simple shroud.

Elisa took out Papa's goose quill pen and inkwell, both now dry. She held the pen in her hands and breathed in the familiar aroma of the ink. That one scent seemed to stimulate more. Soon she also smelled Brazilwood, and nuts, and ocean breezes all rolled together. She smelled Papa. Then she knew there was also a third reason to come to the attic alone. It was time for her to have a really good cry.

* * *

Elisa entered the crowded kitchen a half-hour later and tried to blend in with everyone else. Cecile caught her eye across the room and looked at her with upraised eyebrows. "Did you find it?" she mouthed silently. Elisa shook her head and Cecile made her way through the crowd to her sister.

"You didn't find it?" she asked again.

"No. I found all the things from Papa's office in Pernambuco though."

"So that's why your eyes are so puffy," Cecile said. She gave her sister a hug and encouraged her to take some cheese, bread, and sausage to eat.

Elisa took a plate of food she knew she wouldn't be able to swallow and walked through the foyer. She noticed the basket Mama had put out on a side table to hold the postcards and telegrams the family received. It was much fuller than it had been that morning.

Most of the messages were written in French or Portuguese, and Elisa realized with some surprise that the languages that had once seemed so familiar were beginning to look strange to her now. *They can't bring Papa back no matter what language they are written in*, she thought.

"Bertie won't play dolls with me," Adele sobbed when she saw Elisa come into the dining room. Elisa went over to her little sister, who was sitting all alone in the corner of the room. She knew the real reason for the tears, so she just held Adele close and let her cry.

When the sobbing subsided, Elisa said, "There's someone else who does want your company right now."

"Who is it?" Adele asked, wiping her face with Elisa's linen napkin.

"Come on, I'll show you."

Elisa took Adele by the hand and led her down the hall toward Mama and Papa's bedroom. Just as she suspected, Turk was lying on Papa's side of the bed, his head on his front paws, just as he had been since Papa died. *He looks the way I feel inside*, Elisa thought.

"Ohhh, Turk is so sad," Adele said as she crawled up on the bed and peered into the half-closed eyes of the beloved pet. "I'll stay here with him. He'll be all right again, Lizzie. You'll see."

Elisa left the two youngest members of the family alone to comfort one another. When she checked on them a few minutes later, Adele's head was on top of Turk's, and they were both sound asleep. She covered them with one of Mama's quilts and closed the bedroom door.

As Elisa came back down the hallway she heard Emmanuel offering to hang up Reverend Chavannes' hat. The men were back from the cemetery.

"The Lord is surely washing us clean with this rain," Reverend Chavannes said. "We haven't seen rain like this in the four years we've been here."

Uncle Esperandieu and Emmanuel also tried to get out of some of their wet clothes, but it was impossible for them to get dry. Elisa heard Emmanuel tell her mother that the men had to dip water out of Papa's grave before they could lower the coffin into it. She decided the abundance of water was just God's way of letting them know that He understood how deep their grief truly was. He was a compassionate God. He had emptied heaven of all its tears.

*   *   *

The next day the rain turned to freezing pellets that peppered the windowpanes. Elisa couldn't imagine a weather condition more suited to the family's mood. It was miserable, and so were they.

Mama busied herself in the kitchen, putting away the leftover food and then getting it out again. Every so often she would sit at the kitchen table and read some of the condolences. When she got to one that made her cry, then she went back to stacking spoons or stirring soup.

"It was a nice service, wasn't it?" Mama said to anyone who passed through the kitchen. "Papa would be pleased, don't you think?"

Elisa, Cecile, Emmanuel, Albertine, Adele and Turk just tried to remember what it was they did before Papa died. Nothing was the same. No one wanted to play checkers, because Papa had taught them. No one wanted to read a book for fear they might read about some privileged child who still had a father. The days seemed endless.

After three days, two things happened. The rain stopped, and Mama decided it was time for the children to go back to school. Aunt Cecile arranged to come spend a few days with Mama and Adele so they wouldn't feel too alone.

Elisa knew going back to school would be hard. The first day, it did seem as if everyone was looking at the four Bolli children and pitying them. At recess, when she saw someone walking toward her she wanted to run before they could mention Papa. She managed to keep from crying unless someone said, "I'm so sorry your father died." Then all she could do was nod and walk away.

After being back at school for a week or so, however, Elisa found she was actually beginning to think about her studies again. The teacher talked about the North Pole and the South Pole and asked the children to imagine what it would be like to be on an expedition to one of those exotic points. It was just the distraction the Bolli children needed. Still, Elisa felt guilty when she let even a few minutes pass without thinking about Papa.

Elisa only occasionally took her Bible to school to read aloud from the New Testament before Papa died, but after Papa died she kept her Bible and her journal with her always. The Bible gave her words of comfort to remind her that she would be with Papa again someday. The journal became a place to record all the fears and doubts in her heart so that she could pray about them.

Walking back and forth to school in the cold was the only exercise the children got in the winter. "Remember how it felt to walk in the deep sand on the beach in Pernambuco?" Elisa asked Cecile one day as they struggled to make it up the last part of the road to the farm. "That's how it feels to walk since Papa died. Like I can't move my feet at all."

"That's just how it feels, Lizzie," Cecile said. "You always put into words what I'm feeling too. I would feel so alone without you."

* * *

February eventually turned to March. Turk began to leave the bedroom more often and was even curling up in the kitchen after going outside instead of returning to his spot on the bed. The first warm day, Elisa decided it was time for the first hike of spring. She took Turk and her Bible with her.

It was both unsettling and comforting to be back in the familiar woods. Turk was out of shape after his long winter of grieving, and he began to pant. So Elisa stopped to rest on a rock by the creek. Getting her Bible out of her pack, she turned to Psalm 147 and began to read to Turk, who looked up at her with his head cocked to one side.

"The Lord has been good to us these last few weeks, Turk," Elisa said. She believed the dog's grief was every bit as real as her own. "'He healeth the broken in heart, and bindeth up their wounds,' it says in verse 3. That's what he's doing for us all, isn't it, Turk? It takes time, but I know we are being healed."

The community of cousins and friends had been a big part of the healing process for the Bolli family. Mama never had to go more than a couple of days without someone stopping by with food and time for a good chat. The relatives in France and Switzerland, as well as old friends in Brazil, continued to send postcards and letters.

One day when the children came in from school, Mama was more excited than they had seen her in months. "Guess what, children?" Mama said. "My brother, Charlie Porta, is sending his son Albert to live with us for a while. It's an answer to prayer. I've been praying for someone to help us get the spring crops in," Mama said. "It's too much for Emmanuel to do alone, and I'm afraid the rest of us won't be enough help."

The children had never met their cousin, Albert Porta. They knew he was only sixteen and no substitute for Papa. Still, they caught some of Mama's excitement when she began scurrying around getting everything ready for him.

Chapter Twelve

Elisa wondered how Emmanuel felt about Cousin Albert's
coming. She knew Mama told him again and again what a
good job he had done with the farm while Papa was sick.
Mama also told him how important it was for him to stay in
school during planting season. That wouldn't be possible
unless the family had more help.

Still, Elisa couldn't help but wonder if her brother really
wanted Cousin Albert's help. She found the opportunity to
talk to him about it while walking home from school one day.
When Albertine grabbed Cecile's bonnet, just to tease her,
Cecile went running down the road after her sister. This left
Elisa and Emmanuel to walk on alone together.

"How are you really feeling about Cousin Albert's coming?" she asked.

"What do you mean?" Emmanuel replied.

"I just can't help but think you might be feeling out of
sorts or something. After all, you've learned a lot about the
farm this year. I think you've been doing a great job. Do you
really think you need Cousin Albert's help?"

"Thanks for believing in me, Elisa," Emmanuel said. "But
you don't know how much work is involved in putting in the
crops. I was really worried that Mama was going to spend a
lot of the money Papa left us on seed, and then I would plant
it wrong and lose everything."

"So you're glad Cousin Albert is coming?"

"All I know is that the Porta family has a huge farm in
Switzerland. Albert has been helping his father for years. If
you remember, our family barely knew a rooster from a hen

when we moved here. And do you remember when I let the corn get too coarse before picking it? I have to believe Cousin Albert can teach us all a thing or two about farming," Emmanuel said.

"I'm glad to hear you feel that way, since he's already coming," Elisa said.

"The sooner he gets here, the better, Elisa. Maybe now I'll have time to go with you on some of your hikes," Emmanuel said. "I'll bring my fishing rod and see if there are really trout in that creek."

* * *

A few days later, Cousin Albert arrived. Mama was fixing supper when she heard a knock on the front door. When she opened it, she saw a tall, gangly young man wearing knickers too short for him and a well-worn cap. At his feet was a cloth valise with leather handles.

"*Madame Bolli?*" he said to Mama. "*Je suis Albert* (I am Albert)."

Mama gave Cousin Albert a huge hug and immediately brought him into the kitchen. "Let me look at you," she said. "Oh my, you look so much like your father did at your age. Please, sit down. How did you get out to our farm? Did you hitch a ride with one of the neighbors?"

"No, Madame," Cousin Albert replied. "I walked from the train station."

"That can't be! You must be just exhausted. How I wish we had been there to meet you when you got off the train. If only I had known when you were coming."

"It was good for me to walk," Cousin Albert said. "It gave me a chance to see other farms on the way."

Just then Emmanuel came through the back door carrying an armful of wood for the fireplace. He knew without being told that this must be Cousin Albert. So he quickly dropped the wood into the wood box and walked across the kitchen with his hand extended.

Cousin Albert rose to his feet and grasped Emmanuel's hand in his own.

"Welcome, Cousin," Emmanuel said.

"*Merci*, Cousin," Cousin Albert responded.

The two young men stood almost eye to eye, with Cousin Albert just a bit taller but much slimmer than Emmanuel. Cousin Albert looked wiry but strong, and Emmanuel could almost begin to feel the weight he had carried for so long being gently lifted from his shoulders. Mama sensed the relief in her son.

"Let me give you boys a piece of pie and some milk," Mama said as she wiped her eyes with her apron. "Then you can show Cousin Albert the farm, Emmanuel."

*   *   *

"There isn't much that I can tell you that you don't already know," Emmanuel said as he started the tour of the farm a few minutes later. "This is the barn, and that log shed is where I keep all the tools. Over there is the hen house."

"And where do you keep the horses?" Cousin Albert asked.

"We don't have a horse yet," Emmanuel said. He noticed a shocked and concerned look on Cousin Albert's face.

"But don't worry, we can borrow a team to do the plowing."

"*C'est bon*," Cousin Albert said as a look of relief crossed his face. He was ready to work hard in exchange for room and board in America, but he had never had to pull a plow himself in Switzerland.

"Tomorrow I need to mend the fence row," Emmanuel said. "You can come with me and see the fields then. I've started on the planting, but it's not too late to get your advice. I have so much to learn."

"It is my pleasure to share with you what the good Lord has allowed me to learn," Cousin Albert said.

Emmanuel turned to look straight into Cousin Albert's face.

"Thank you for coming so far to help us," he said.

"It is the will of the Lord," Cousin Albert responded. "When the Holy Spirit tells us to go, we must go."

Emmanuel stretched out his hand again, but this time the handshake was followed by a hug. Then the two young men turned to go back to the kitchen to visit with Mama until dinner.

At the dinner table, Elisa and Cecile had a million questions for Cousin Albert. They wanted to talk to him in French so he would understand them more quickly, but Mama reminded them that Cousin Albert really wanted to learn English. "You would do him a favor to ask him questions in English," she said.

"Where do your sisters go to school in Lausanne?" Elisa asked. "Are their studies very hard?"

"They go to religious school," Cousin Albert said. "The studies are, how do you say, *difficile*, no? But my sisters think more about the boys and the cotillions."

"Just like us!" Cecile laughed.

Albertine and Adele wanted to ask Cousin Albert questions, too, but they were too shy. They peeked at him while he talked, but as soon as he looked their way, they lowered their heads and giggled.

"These little ones resemble my younger cousins in Switzerland," Cousin Albert said. "Petite dark eyes dancing with merriment." He smiled at them and winked.

* * *

In the next few days, Cousin Albert helped Emmanuel with the planting and everyone helped Cousin Albert feel more at home. Mama even gave him some of Papa's clothes to wear. At first Elisa thought it was strange to see someone else in Papa's clothes, but Mama said it was the sensible thing to do. She said she thought Cousin Albert had a lot more growth in him, anyway. He wouldn't be able to wear Papa's clothes for long.

Elisa took it upon herself to help Cousin Albert with his English. She wrote up vocabulary lessons and held class at the kitchen table after the dishes were cleared away. With Emmanuel reinforcing what Elisa taught Cousin Albert as the two worked together during the day, Cousin Albert was soon able to discuss farm business easily in English as well as in French. Teaching him made Elisa realize how much she and the other Bolli children had learned in less than a year.

March not only brought Cousin Albert to the Bolli farm, it also brought the first signs of spring to the rolling green hills, forests, and meadows of East Tennessee.

At first, Elisa didn't want to see the purple violets peeking up at her from the forest floor when she went on her walks. It seemed wrong that something as wonderful as spring would come into a world without Papa.

One afternoon Elisa was crying as she returned to the back yard. Cousin Albert was sitting on the back porch cleaning mud off his boots. Elisa tried to slip by without his noticing her tears, but he reached out and touched her arm as she went by.

"Cousin Elisa, you have the tears in the eyes," he said. "Why do you cry today?"

"Oh, Albert," Elisa sobbed. "I just don't understand how spring can happen all around us. Papa's dead, but the world just goes on as if nothing has happened."

"Ah, I see," Albert said. "That is very difficult. But, Elisa, the Bible says there is a time for everything. This is the time for spring."

"I guess it is, Albert."

"Spring will help you to heal your heart. You will see."

Elisa didn't really understand how spring could be healing, but that night she prayed. She asked the Lord to help her understand her feelings. Reading in her Bible the next morning, Elisa sensed the Lord answering her prayer through a verse she discovered in Song of Solomon. There she read,

"For, lo, the winter is past, the rain is over and gone; The flowers appear on the earth; the time of the singing of birds is come . . ."

Elisa thought about the cold winter the family had experienced. She could almost feel the bone-chilling dampness of the January rains that would always remind her of Papa's death. She realized then that Cousin Albert was right. Spring was a gift from the Lord. It was a way He could assure Elisa and her family that life could go on without Papa. It was the Lord's way of saying that He would never leave them, but always protect and bless them as part of His wonderful creation.

Once she understood, Elisa wanted to share the blessing of spring with the rest of her family. When she noticed the first buds on the yellow forsythia bush in the yard, she cut a handful of branches and brought them inside. She put the branches in a vase filled with warm water from the tea kettle and set the vase on the kitchen windowsill in the sun. The buds became tiny yellow flowers in no time.

When Mama came into the kitchen and saw the forsythia she began to cry, and Elisa quickly realized it was because Papa always used to cut flowers from the garden in Brazil and bring them inside to surprise his wife.

"I'm sorry, Mama," Elisa said, crying herself. "I didn't mean to make you cry. I just wanted to bring you a bit of spring from the yard."

"It was a lovely thought, honey, and the forsythia is beautiful. I just miss your Papa so much. Don't worry about my tears. They are healing the sadness in my soul," Mama said.

Soon it was April, and spring was in full bloom. The woods were full of clusters of mountain laurel blossoms and the sweet fragrance of lily-of-the-valley. The dogwood trees danced gracefully across the hillsides dressed in their lacy pink and white blossoms.

When Emma came for a weekend visit, she brought plants

and seedlings from her parents' gardens. She and Elisa spent most of one Saturday digging and planting a flower bed on the south side of the house. "What did you say these flowers were called again?" Elisa asked Emma as she patted the soil around a bushy plant covered with star-shaped pink blossoms.

"Impatiens," Emma replied.

"Well, I'll be impatient to see how all this turns out," Elisa laughed.

"I thought all kinds of flowers grew in Brazil, Elisa," Emma said. "Didn't you learn all the names when you planted your gardens there?"

"Mama knew all the names of the plants but I really didn't," Elisa said. "We hired gardeners to plant the gardens. Now I see how much fun I missed."

"Well as long as we get plenty of rain, this garden should grow quickly," Emma said. "The clumps of daisies we planted behind these impatiens will grow taller than they are. Those roses behind the daisies will grow taller still. And the little clumps of English Ivy we planted right next to the house will begin to climb soon. By this time next year, ivy should just about cover the side of your house."

"And I'll be able to send you home with a bouquet every time you visit," Elisa said.

"How pretty this looks," Mama said as she joined the girls in the side yard.

"Thank you so much for bringing the plants, Emma."

"You are very welcome, Mrs. Bolli. My mother says flowers make a cloudy day sunny," Emma said.

"And so they do," Mama agreed. "When you girls are finished, come join me in the parlor. I want to show you something else pretty."

When Elisa and Emma entered the parlor an hour or so later, they saw Mama sitting in the new walnut rocker Cousin Albert had made for her. He had started woodworking in the evenings to help Mama furnish the house, and he was getting very skillful at it. Mama had pulled the rocker over to the window and was working on a beautiful quilt square. The design featured an eight-pointed star the color of blue sky on a soft white background.

"Isn't this a lovely design?" Mama said. "Aunt Esperandieu asked me to finish this square for her. I wanted you to see it, Elisa, because I realize I've been neglecting your instruction in needlework since we moved to America. You girls have barely made any progress at all on your samplers. Now it's time you learned to quilt so we can begin your trousseaus."

At the mention of trousseaus, Elisa and Emma began to giggle. It would only be a few years before they were old enough to be married. Then they would leave home with trunks packed with linens and quilts they had stitched by hand. But that day seemed far away to them now.

"My mother said there's going to be a quilting bee at the Esperandieus next Saturday," Emma said. "Are you going, Mrs. Bolli?"

"Yes, I am," Mama said. "Elisa, you and Cecile are invited, too, if you'd like to come."

Elisa looked forward to Saturdays because they gave her a chance to take longer walks through the woods and climb up the ridge to see the mountains in the distance. But she didn't want to miss being with Emma and the Esperandieu girls. Besides, when she spent time with her mother, Aunt Cecile, and the other women, she felt a special sense of belonging. Hearing them talk about cooking meals for their families, birthing babies, and understanding their husbands helped Elisa come to know what being a woman was all about.

Soon school would be out for the summer and she could go on all the long hikes she wanted. She would go to the quilting bee.

"Say you'll come," urged Emma. "Maybe you could even spend the night with me afterward and stay through services on Sunday!"

"I'll be there!" Elisa said. "Was that all you wanted us for, Mama?" Elisa asked.

"Yes, dear. You're excused."

"Come on then, Emma," Elisa said. "Let's go on a hike."

*   *   *

The quilting bee was a wonderful success. Not only did the group finish a quilt for one of the cousins who was getting married, they consumed trays full of ginger cakes, cookies, and other sweet treats, and drank gallons of lemonade.

Elisa was a bit disappointed, however, when she learned that she, Cecile, and the other young girls couldn't sit side-by-side. Rather, they were positioned in between experienced quilters around the quilt frame so that they could receive instruction as they stitched.

"Those stitches are a bit too long, dear," Mrs. Buffat whispered to Elisa in the middle of a discussion about the new pastor expected to arrive any day at Spring Place Presbyterian Church. "Take them out and try again."

Elisa looked across the stretched quilt, now a sea of blue stars on foamy white cotton cloth, to catch Emma's eye. Emma's expression didn't have much sympathy in it, however. She'd just had to repeat a whole row of stitches herself.

"I'll never get married if I have to make a pile of these quilts first," Elisa commented to Emma and Cecile during a lemonade break.

"Maybe we'll each be fortunate enough to marry a widower," Emma laughed. "Then we'll just inherit his first wife's trousseau!"

Chapter Thirteen

By the time May arrived it was almost too hot to go to school. The windows and doors of the log schoolhouse were kept open all day long in an attempt to lure inside any breeze that happened by. This made it necessary for the teacher to move among the students with a fly swatter to keep the flies, bees, and mosquitoes under control.

Just when Elisa would be close to having the answer to one of her arithmetic problems about the number of apples left in a bushel, or about making change at the dry goods store, a loud "Swat!" would ruin her concentration and she'd have to start over.

Writing May dates in her journal made Elisa think about her birthday to come—and her last birthday. Could it really have been almost a year since her last shopping trip with Papa in Pernambuco? In some ways that day didn't seem long ago at all. But when Elisa thought about all the family had been through since moving to America, she realized it had been a very long year after all.

"I don't really need anything for my birthday, Mama," Elisa announced at breakfast in the middle of May. "I know you have to spend money on the farm. Please don't worry about getting me a gift."

"Oh, really?" Mama teased. "Well, we'll just have to see about that, won't we?"

On the morning of May 18, Elisa spent extra time getting dressed for school. There would be an awards program that day and she fully expected to win the award for best penmanship. The prize was a collection of poetry by Samuel Taylor

Coleridge and a set of goose quill pens—more than enough to get her through the summer.

Elisa chose a calico dress with pink flowers and tied a pink ribbon in the back of her hair so everyone would see it when she walked forward to accept her award. That's when she realized she was feeling very prideful.

"Forgive me, Lord," she prayed before going downstairs. "I know every good gift comes from You, including any talent I have. If I win an award today, let it be to Your glory, not mine."

"Surprise! Happy birthday!" everyone yelled when Elisa finally came into the kitchen for breakfast. Next to her place stood a small walnut bookcase with two shelves that Cousin Albert had made.

"Happy birthday, Cousin Elisa," Cousin Albert said with hardly a hint of a French accent. "For your twelfth birthday, a case for your books."

"Oh, Albert! It's beautiful! I love it!" Elisa said. Then she noticed the presents everyone else had piled on her chair and hurried to open them before leaving for school.

First there was a new journal from Cecile, one that she had been given but hadn't used yet. Elisa had admired it for ages.

"Oh, Cile! Are you sure you don't want this yourself?" Elisa squealed when she saw it.

"I want you to have it more, Lizzie. Happy birthday."

"Thank you so much."

"My gift is that I'm going to do your chores all week," Emmanuel piped in.

"Those are both great gifts—and they go together!" Elisa said. "Now I'll have time to write in my new journal."

The largest gift was from Mama. It was lumpy and bulky. When Elisa tore open the wrapping, she saw a beautiful soft yellow and white blanket her mother had knitted for her. The pattern was the same one Mama had used for a blanket she had made for Cecile several years before.

"Oh, Mama! It's beautiful. When did you have time to do this?"

"I completed most of it while I sat up with Papa at night. We both wanted you to have it for your trousseau," Mama said.

"I'll treasure it always—and I'll never lose it. I promise!"

"Open our present, Lizzie! Open ours!" Albertine cried out.

"Yes, hurry!" Adele added.

The package made a crunchy sound when Elisa picked it up.

"Whatever could this be?" she wondered.

Inside were two dolls made of cornhusks. They had dried apples for heads and raisins for eyes. Each was wearing a pinafore the girls had fashioned out of some of Mama's sewing scraps.

"These are wonderful!" Elisa said. "They make me happy just looking at them. Thank you, sisters!"

The rest of the day went as well as it had begun. Elisa did win the award. When she got home, she put the slim volume of Coleridge poetry right on the new bookcase that Cousin Albert had carried up to her bedroom. That evening, Mama surprised Elisa with a round birthday cake with real flowers on top, and after supper the girls danced around in the yard like fairies.

Elisa was sad that Papa wasn't with her on her birthday this year, but reading her Bible that day at school helped her feel closer to him. "So teach us to number our days," she read in Psalm 90, "that we may apply our hearts unto wisdom."

During math class that day, Elisa decided she would number the days Papa had been alive. First she multiplied forty-nine years by fifty-two weeks, then multiplied that total by seven days per week. Papa died on January 26, just seventeen days before his fiftieth birthday on February 12, so she subtracted seventeen from 365 and added that to the total.

"I know Your ways are higher than our ways, Lord," she said in her prayers that night. "But I'll never understand why You gave someone as good as Papa only 18,184 days to live on this earth."

* * *

The last day of school was one of mixed emotions for Elisa. She loved the thought of free time, longer days, and warm evenings on the front porch watching her sisters chase after lightnin' bugs. Still, she knew she would miss seeing her friends every day. At least this summer she knew lots of people.

"I hope you'll be coming to all the youth activities at the Presbyterian church this summer," Alfred Buffat said to her at recess. "The elders voted to allow us to have dances too. We're even going to learn the Virginia reel."

The whole time Alfred was talking to her, Elisa was trying not to look at his head. He had always had such nice hair, trimmed so it covered the tops of his ears, and with a lock of dark curls in the middle of his forehead. Now Alfred's hair was cut so close it almost looked like his head had been shaved. Finally Elisa's curiosity got the best of her.

"Forgive me for asking, Alfred," Elisa began, "but what happened to your hair? Was there an outbreak of head lice at your house, or do you always have shorter hair in the summer?"

"Neither one," Alfred blushed. "My father caught me taking particular pains styling my hair in front of the looking glass. He said I was being far too vain and that he knew the perfect remedy. I had to sit on a stool in the front yard while he cropped off all my hair."

"Well, I'm sure it will grow back nicely," Elisa managed to say. She was glad to hear the teacher calling the pupils back inside so she could turn away from Albert before he saw that she was trying not to laugh. Then Elisa remembered her own vanity the day of the awards ceremony. She said a silent prayer for Alfred.

* * *

In late May, Elisa watched the buds on the magnolia trees closely so she could bring the first blossom she saw inside to Mama. By the time the magnolia trees burst into bloom, filling the night air with their intoxicating fragrance as their giant blossoms glowed in the moonlight, Emmanuel and Cousin Albert were already seeing ears of corn forming on the stalks and tiny green beans on the vines.

Then it was time for Cousin Albert to show Emmanuel how to cut the hay. The girls helped rake it into rows with hand rakes. Then it was forked into stacks pitched onto the hay wagon to be hauled to the barn. Elisa thought the smell of fresh mown hay was every bit as wonderful as the fragrance of the magnolia blossoms. She hoped she would never have to miss spring in Tennessee, and she was sorry she ever questioned the Lord for sending it. After all, spring gave birth to summer.

With the crops doing well, and the family beginning to recover from the trauma of losing Papa, Mama announced that she and the girls would be able to make several weekend visits during the summer.

Elisa was delighted. Especially since the first visit would be to the Chavannes farm and she would get to see Emma. The plan was to stop for Mary and Lily Esperandieu on the way. Elisa was especially excited about Lily bringing her pony.

The first Friday in June, Mama packed a basket with two loaves of homemade bread and a strawberry pie made with the first berries of summer. Just Cecile and Elisa were going with Mama this time. The younger girls were staying home with Emmanuel and Cousin Albert.

The girls packed their nightclothes in the satchel with Mama's nightclothes and knitting. Then with Elisa carrying the basket and Cecile carrying the satchel, the threesome started down the dusty road.

What a merry group they were after they left the

Esperandieus. Mama didn't want to ride, so the girls took turns on Lily's pony. When it was Elisa's turn, she set off at a gallop. Being out in front of the group made her feel like performing.

"Yippee! Look at me!" Elisa called out. "I'm a circus showgirl!"

Elisa had seen showgirls at a circus in Knoxville that she had attended with her classmates. Like them, she rode for a while with the reins in her teeth and her hands in the air. Then she stood up in the stirrups.

"Bet you can't do this, Cile!" she called, as she put all her weight on her left foot and stuck her right foot straight out behind her. She rode standing in the saddle, then kneeling, and finally kneeling backward, much to the delight of most of the audience behind her.

"Please be careful, dear!" Mama shouted over the sound of the girls' laughter.

When it was time for Elisa to dismount and let Cecile have a turn, she wanted to do it with flair, so she attempted to jump from the saddle to the ground. But on the way down her skirt caught on the saddle horn, and Elisa flipped around and fell onto the dirt road, landing hard on her right elbow.

"Oh, my arm!" Elisa cried out. "It hurts so much. I can't move it!"

The fall dislocated Elisa's elbow and split the bone. She couldn't lift her arm to look at it, but she knew it was bent in the wrong direction. The look on Mama's face told her all she needed to know. Suddenly Elisa noticed that all the faces looking down at her were swimming around in a circle. Then she fainted.

While Elisa was unconscious, Mama pulled on her arm to try to get it back into joint, but it still wasn't right. By the time she came to, the arm was badly swollen.

"Cecile, get your nightdress out of the satchel," Mama said. "Let's see if we can make a sling out of it." Working together,

Mama and the girls managed to get Elisa up on the pony behind Lily. They took her on to the Chavannes farm since they were almost there when the accident happened.

As soon as they arrived, Albert Chavannes rode to fetch Dr. Clark.

By the time Dr. Clark arrived, Emma and Mrs. Chavannes had helped Mama and Cecile get Elisa into bed. She looked so pale surrounded by all the white feather pillows they had piled behind her head and under her hurt arm.

"So we have an injured showgirl here, do we?" Dr. Clark said when he entered the room with his black leather bag. Elisa hadn't seen Dr. Clark since Papa died, and she actually wondered if she was dying now too. *If so, at least I'll be with Papa again,* she thought.

Dr. Clark tried to be as gentle as possible as he took Elisa's hand and pulled on her arm to straighten it out, but she screamed in pain.

"I'm sorry to hurt you, dear," the doctor said. "I'm just trying to discover the extent of the injury. I'm going to order cold compresses for a few days to get the swelling down, then I'll be back to look at the arm again."

"Do you think her elbow is back in place, Dr. Clark?" Mama asked as she gently patted Elisa's forehead to calm her. "We heard a snap when I pulled on it, but I'm concerned that I may not have done it right."

"You were brave to try to set it at all, Mrs. Bolli," Dr. Clark said. "We'll know more when the swelling goes down. I have an apparatus that can help us straighten the arm out more if need be. For now, I think we should just let her rest and wait to see how much healing occurs naturally."

Mama showed Dr. Clark out while Mrs. Chavannes, Emma, Cecile, Lily, and Mary hovered around Elisa. This gave Mama a chance to talk with the doctor alone, but she didn't learn anything more except that the injury was definitely a serious one.

"Dr. Clark says we shouldn't move her for at least ten days," Mama announced when she came back into the bedroom. "I'm afraid we've created quite an inconvenience for you," she said to Mrs. Chavannes.

"Nonsense," Mrs. Chavannes said. "You know you are welcome to stay here as long as necessary. Having you here will make it easier for Emma and me to help you take care of Elisa. And we can pray together for her healing."

"You're so kind. I'm afraid we have no other choice. Thank you so much," Mama said.

"Cecile, I'll stay here with Elisa until we can move her," Mama continued. "You should go home with Lily and Mary and let the rest of our family know what happened. Tell them Elisa is going to be fine. She just needs some time to recover."

"Then I'm not dying?" Elisa asked with a weak voice.

"No, dear. Not this time," Mama laughed. "But you might want to be a bit more careful in the future."

Elisa was in a great deal of pain, and she was very upset about ruining the visit to the Chavannes.

"Oh, Emma, I messed up all our plans to take hikes and ride horses together this summer," Elisa said. "I'm so sorry."

"Don't be silly, Elisa," Emma said. "And lie still. I'm supposed to be keeping these cold compresses on your arm."

Emma stayed up night after night to help Mama care for Elisa. Finally, when Elisa was able to travel, Reverend Chavannes took her and her mother home in his buggy.

Dr. Clark paid regular visits to the Bolli farm to check on Elisa. He was concerned that her arm remained so crooked, so on one of the visits he brought the apparatus for straightening her elbow. Elisa couldn't believe it was actually going to be put on her arm when she first saw it. There were metal cuffs to go around her upper arm and her lower arm. Metal rods attached the cuffs to a padded, metal cup that fit over her elbow. The rods were attached to the elbow cup, which had a large metal screw sticking out of it.

"That looks like some medieval torture system I've seen in the history text at school," Elisa said when Dr. Clark first showed her the apparatus.

"I know, dear, but if you twist the screw gently every day, the change in your arm will be gradual and it shouldn't hurt. You may take the apparatus off an hour a day to bathe, but I want you to wear it all the rest of the time, even to sleep, until the screw is all the way into the metal cup here," Dr. Clark explained. "That tightens the rods which force your arm to straighten out.".

Cecile, Albertine, and Adele all helped keep Elisa company during her long recuperation. Cecile went to one of the youth gatherings at Spring Place Presbyterian Church that Alfred had told Elisa about on the last day of school. She told her sister all about it when she got home.

"You'll love the Virginia reel," Cecile said as she sat on Elisa's bed to tell her about the dance. "It's kind of like the cotillions and quadrilles we know, but the music's a lot more lively. We even had fiddles! You take the hand of the boy opposite you and then you pull one another through the square."

"Oh, no!" Elisa groaned as she grabbed her sore arm. "Now I know I'm not going!"

After a while Elisa was allowed to get out of bed. By the Fourth of July, she felt well enough to ride in the back of a wagon with her cousins to the parade in Knoxville. Her arm hurt the whole day, and she didn't do much flag-waving, but she did get to see the horses in their fancy saddles and all the clowns and musicians.

The town was so colorful. Everyone had red, white, and blue festoons hanging on their front porches. An American flag hung from every lamppost on Gay Street. The French-Swiss children had studied the American Revolution at Spring Place School, so they knew all about Independence Day. The highlight of the day, July 4, 1854, was the arrival of Knoxville's first train.

Elisa was crowded into the back of the Esperandieus' wagon with the other children. Cecile sat on her right side to protect her injured arm.

"I can't see, Cile," Elisa complained. "I think I hear the train, but I can't see anything."

"I see the steam from the engine in the distance," Cecile said. "Come on. I'll help you stand up so you can see better."

"That looks like the same train we took from Savannah to Loudon on our trip from Brazil," Elisa said when the train screeched to a halt and blew its whistle. The crowd cheered wildly.

"It could be," Cile yelled over the shouting. "But I imagine they all look quite a bit alike."

"It's exciting to think about coming straight here by train instead of having to take the stagecoach from Loudon to Knoxville," Elisa said. "I wish Papa could see this. He would be so excited."

"Me, too, Lizzie," Cecile said. "Just think—when we're older, we could leave right from here by train and see all of America—even New York City!"

"Right now, I just want to sit down again," Elisa said, and Cecile helped her back down onto the wagon bed.

After seeing the train, the families gathered at the Esperandieus for a picnic on the grounds. The children took turns cranking the homemade ice cream. Elisa didn't have to crank because of her elbow, but she got to eat some of the creamy vanilla ice cream just the same.

Even though Elisa was careful to tighten the screw each day as Dr. Clark had instructed, the apparatus failed to straighten her arm completely. Finally, at the beginning of August, Dr. Clark determined that Elisa would just have to learn to live with a crooked arm and he told her she could stop wearing the dreadful apparatus. To make her feel better about the situation, he also told her she could resume her walks, but only if she was very careful not to fall. She had to leave Turk behind for fear he would accidentally trip her.

Elisa was determined to put the accident behind her, and she worked hard at learning to write again after not being able to use her arm for so long. Over and over she copied the inscription Papa had written in his strong hand in the front of her Bible. *Elisa Bolli—Donné par son cher Papa—Mai 18, 1853.* Just seeing Papa's handwriting inspired her to keep trying. By the end of the summer, she felt her penmanship had almost returned to its award-winning form.

She also did a lot of talking to God. Elisa didn't understand why something else bad had to happen just when the family was beginning to recover from Papa's death. One Sunday when the Chavannes family stopped by to visit, she asked Reverend Chavannes if God was punishing her for her vanity, or for showing off in front of her friends.

"You hurt your elbow because you fell off the pony," Reverend Chavannes said. "That's the beginning and the end of it. The Lord Jesus told us we would have trouble in this world. But He promised to be with us through the trouble. And He has been with you through yours."

Elisa knew this was true. She had felt the Lord's presence as she grieved for Papa. She knew He had also helped her elbow to heal and given her the strength to hike and write again. Taking the truth Reverend Chavannes showed her into her heart helped Elisa accept the pain she had been through, and the pain that was to come.

* * *

In August, Elisa was also able to go to several of the dances at Spring Place Presbyterian Church. She learned to do the Virginia reel, and the boys were very careful not to hurt her bad arm.

All the way home from a dance one night, Elisa and Cecile giggled about being squared off with Alfred Buffat and Albert Chavannes. Emmanuel and Cousin Albert had gone to the dance too. They were escorting the girls home in the dark,

112

but following at a safe distance to avoid the giggling.

Suddenly, the girls screamed and began running for home.

"What's the matter with you two?" Emmanuel called after them.

"It's a bat!" Elisa cried. "It's diving at us!"

"He's probably more afraid of you than you are of him," Emmanuel called when he saw the dark, bird-like shape zipping through the night sky.

Chapter Fourteen

It had gotten harder and harder to keep Turk in the yard once he got over grieving for Papa. Emmanuel even tried tying him to a tree in the backyard, but he bit through the rope and went on one of his adventures.

When Turk came home one day at suppertime, Mama noticed that his black and white coat was matted with mud. She didn't know what he had been into, but she knew it wasn't good. She wasn't surprised when a new neighbor from up the road stopped by to tell her to keep her dog at home.

"That fool dog's been after my hogs," Mr. Johnson yelled at Mama through the front door without even getting down off his wagon. "If I see him on my property again, I'm going to shoot him."

Emmanuel planned to buy stonger rope for tying Turk up in the yard on his next trip to town. But just two days later, Mama was getting supper ready when she heard a gunshot, followed by Albertine screaming at the top of her lungs.

Her heart was in her throat as she ran to the front porch. The family only owned one gun, and Emmanuel always kept it locked up. What could have happened? Then she remembered the neighbor's threat.

When she came out onto the porch, she saw the neighbor's wagon going down the lane. Then she saw Turk lying at the bottom of the stairs, right at Albertine's feet, in a pool of blood.

As sad as it would have been for Turk to die on the spot, it might have been better for him and easier on the family if he had. Instead, he lingered for days. Mama dressed the wound in his shoulder where the bullet had passed clean through, and Adele and Albertine took turns sleeping next to him at night. The third day, Mama called a family meeting.

"This is hard for me to say," Mama began. "But I think we all know Turk is in a lot of pain. He isn't even lifting his head anymore. He just lies there and whimpers. We love him too much to see him go on like this."

"Do you want me to put him out of his misery, Mama?" Emmanuel asked with a lump in his throat.

"That would be too painful for you, but it has to be done," Mama said to Emmanuel. "Go fetch Uncle Theodore and ask him to do it for us."

Elisa thought she would never be able to stop crying. First Papa, and now Turk. She and Cecile wanted to comfort Albertine and Adele as they cuddled with them in their room, but they couldn't control their own sobbing. It wasn't long before they heard another gunshot, and Elisa knew Turk would never run through the woods with her again.

Never did a dog have a funeral like Turk's. Cousin Albert built a walnut coffin for him from some of his woodworking scraps. Albertine and Adele wove roses and ivy into a blanket for the top of the coffin. Emmanuel dug a hole under an apple tree in the backyard, and Cousin Albert lowered the coffin into it. Then the family gathered around for Turk's funeral.

Mama began the service by reading a verse from 1 Thessalonians. "'In every thing give thanks: for this is the will of God in Christ Jesus concerning you.'" Then Mama prayed, "Lord, we are sad to lose our faithful dog, Turk. But we remember to give You thanks for him, and for all the joy he brought to us.

"We are also thankful that Albertine was not hurt when Turk was shot, Lord," Mama continued. "That would have been a grief so hard for us to bear. Through all our losses, we know that Your grace is sufficient for us, and we give You thanks."

Next it was time for Elisa to play the accordion and lead

everyone in the singing of a hymn for Turk. Her stiff elbow made it hard to play, but she wanted to do it for Turk.

"Let's all sing 'Fairest Lord Jesus,'" Elisa said as she played the introductory notes. "It talks about meadows and woodlands—two of the places Turk so loved to explore."

After the hymn, the children took turns shoveling dirt on top of the coffin and saying good-bye to Turk, the best dog ever.

*   *   *

That night when Elisa crawled into bed she thought back on the day and on the funeral for Turk. The heavy, familiar feelings of grief came over her again. How much she would miss seeing Turk running through the fall leaves again. How strange it would be not to find him curled up by the fireplace in the kitchen next winter.

But when she thought about the service, it was the image of her mother that wouldn't leave her mind. Mama, standing straight and tall by Turk's grave. Mama, knowing just the Scripture verse to read and just the words to pray to bring comfort to the hearts of her grieving children.

I don't remember Mama being so strong before, Elisa thought. *How has she had the strength to run the farm without Papa? Besides that, she didn't even hesitate when she had to pull my dislocated arm back into place. And she nursed me back to health without ever once saying, "I told you to be careful showing off on that pony." And now, when Turk got shot, it was Mama who made the hard decision to put him out of his misery—and Mama who presided at his funeral just as capably as Papa would have done it.*

Certainly I don't have Mama's courage, Elisa thought. *Cecile and I screamed and ran all the way home because we saw a bat! Another night, I slept in my high-button shoes and clothes because there had been a bat in the attic. Mama wouldn't be afraid of a bat. I'm sure of that.*

The next morning, Elisa was up with the sun. Something told her she needed to get started as early as possible with the rest of her life—life without Papa and Turk.

When she came into the kitchen she saw that her mother was already up for the day too. The coffee was boiling in a kettle hanging over the open fire. Mama was sitting at the kitchen table, her open Bible in front of her.

"You're up bright and early this morning," she said when Elisa came in and joined her at the table. "I'll fix you an early-bird breakfast!"

Elisa watched her mother as she cracked some eggs into a bowl and scrambled them. The sun was just beginning to come in the window and Mama's dark hair shone in the sun's rays. Her hair was pulled straight back into a bun, as it almost always was. Mama seemed trimmer than she had been in Pernambuco. She still looked younger than her forty-two years, in spite of how hard the last year had been on her.

"You're very pensive this morning, daughter," Mama said when she served Elisa her breakfast of scrambled eggs, *saucisson*, and biscuits. "Are you thinking about Turk?"

"Actually, Mama, I've been thinking about you," Elisa said. "We never would have made it through these last months without you, but I know you hurt inside too. How have you been able to do everything you've done for us?"

"The answer to your question, as well as to any other question you'll ever have, is right here," Mama said as she patted her open Bible. "Just this morning I was reading in Nehemiah, and I came across the verse where Nehemiah says to his people, 'The joy of the Lord is your strength.' That's where I get my strength too, Elisa.

"There have been many days when I just wanted to stay in bed and pull the covers over my head, but my love for all of you, and my trust in the Lord, gave me the courage to put my feet on the floor and get up. I hope you'll always remember that. No matter what happens, the Lord will see you through it if you ask Him to."

"Do you think Turk is in heaven with Papa?" Elisa asked.

"The Bible doesn't say whether animals go to heaven, but it's comforting to think of those two being together again, isn't it? I woke up thinking about that this morning myself."

Just then Adele and Albertine came into the kitchen still in their nightclothes. They both tried to climb into Mama's lap at once.

"You girls are getting too big to be lap babies!" Mama said as she struggled not to drop either one of them onto the floor.

"We heard you talking about Turk," Adele said while rubbing the sleep from her eyes. "Bertie thinks we should plant some pansies on his grave, because pansies stand for thoughts—and we'll always think about Turk."

"That's a wonderful idea, girls," Mama said. "And pansies should grow happily in the shade of the apple tree. I'll ask Cousin Albert to get some pansy seeds when he goes to the seed store tomorrow."

When Elisa went on her walk in the woods later that day, she couldn't help thinking about Turk. He had just started going with her on her walks again before he was shot. She kept glancing off the trail, expecting to see him emerging from behind a tree at any minute.

Elisa knew that what Turk did was wrong. She also realized that they were all responsible for not keeping him in the yard. But still, she couldn't help but think that Mr. Johnson had been extremely mean to shoot the family's dog. Especially to do it right in front of Albertine, with no regard for her safety or her feelings.

"Lord, I understand that we must forgive if we are to be forgiven," Elisa prayed aloud as she walked. "But it's just so hard at times. Please help me to love my enemies, even Mr. Johnson, who shot Turk. And as You say, to do good to them that hate us."

When she reached the point where the trail opened up into a meadow, Elisa was greeted by a host of late summer wildflowers in bloom. Walking through waist-deep goldenrod, purple asters, and Queen Anne's lace, she thought the hot summer sun or the goldenrod was making her eyes water. Then she realized that the beauty of the meadow had touched her very soul, and she was crying.

The further she walked, the harder she cried. She cried for Papa, and for her crooked arm that still hurt whenever there was a change in the weather, and she cried for Turk.

Back on the cool woodsy trail again, she noticed a jack-in-the-pulpit poking its head up from among the forest ferns. Of all the flowers, that was the one she picked to take home, because just seeing it made her smile again. It really did look like a preacher standing in a pulpit—a preacher much thinner than Reverend Chavannes.

* * *

When Elisa returned to the house and went up to the room she shared with Cecile, she noticed clothes were lying on both beds.

"Mama wants us to try on our school dresses from last year so she knows what we'll need for next year," Cecile said.

Elisa sat on her bed and watched her sister pull the blue calico dress Mama had made for her down over her head. Cecile lifted her arms and moved them back and forth. Clearly the dress was too tight across the bust. Any jealousy Elisa felt over her sister developing a bustline before she did was eased when she saw the blue dress added to the two already on her bed.

"Mama said she would hem those dresses for you," Cecile said. "You need to try yours on to see what gets passed to Albertine."

Both girls were soon running around the bedroom in their bloomers and camisoles, trying on dresses and enjoying the opportunity to take long looks in the looking glass without feeling too vain. After all, they needed to assess each dress carefully.

"How are you two doing in here?" Mama said at last. "Goodness, me. I have my work cut out for me, don't I?" she said when she saw the three dresses to be hemmed lying on Elisa's bed.

"Mama, I hardly have anything for fall and winter that still fits." Cecile exclaimed. "What am I going to wear to school?"

"I thought that might be the case, dear," Mama said. "But I don't need as many dresses as I did when your father was alive because I don't go out as often. My closet is a good place for us to start rebuilding your wardrobe."

"These two are for Albertine," Elisa said. "They are way up above my ankles. Will you be making any new dresses this fall, Mama?"

"I've ordered the fabric," Mama said. "A bolt of gold percale that Cousin Albert will pick up when he goes to town tomorrow. But the first dress I make is going to be for Adele. With three older sisters she's never had anything but hand-me-downs. I want her to have a brand new dress for her first day of school."

* * *

That night as she was getting ready for bed, Elisa saw the jack-in-the-pulpit she had brought in from her walk still lying on the bedside table where she put it when she began trying on dresses. She pressed it between two pages of her journal. On the next page she wrote: "Taken from the woods on my first walk after Turk's death. I will miss you, my silly, furry friend."

Chapter Fifteen

"We're getting rabbits!" Adele exclaimed when Elisa returned from her walk the next day. "Lots and lots of rabbits!" This was as happy as Elisa had seen her little sister since Turk died.

Mama took a wooden peg out of her mouth and turned from the clothesline where she was hanging clothes to dry. "We're getting two rabbits, Adele, that's all—and I will make sure they are both female!" Mama said.

Elisa realized that her mother was trying to get everyone's mind off Turk. Giving Adele rabbits to care for would distract her. The older girls were to begin learning to make Swiss lace the next morning.

"When, Mama? When will we get the rabbits?" Adele asked.

"After Cousin Albert builds the hutch," Mama answered. "The county fair is in two weeks. I'm sure we can pick out some nice rabbits there."

"Two weeks is too long!" Adele complained.

"All good things are worth waiting for, dear—even rabbits," Mama said. She picked up the laundry basket and went back in the house.

When Elisa came up on the back porch she noticed Albertine reading in the shade. It seemed Albertine was always reading. Elisa wondered if it was her shy sister's way of escaping from the hurts of the past year.

"I sure would like it if you would go with me on my walks, Bertie," Elisa said. "I'm reading *Pilgrim's Progress* now. You can bring one of your primers and I'll bring my book. We can hike up to the meadow and read under a tree. Would you like to do that?"

"I guess so," Albertine said, and Elisa was glad to see that her sister looked more excited than she sounded. She wondered why she hadn't thought to include her before.

Pilgrim's Progress was the most difficult book Elisa had tried to read. Not only did it challenge her mind, but it also spoke to her heart and gave her a yearning to be closer to the Lord. "I am the Lord's and He is mine," she wrote in her journal after reading the first few chapters. "What can I want besides?"

*   *   *

Mama encouraged Cecile, Elisa, and Albertine to finish the lace collars she was teaching them to make in time to enter them in competition at the county fair. Two weeks may have been too long for Adele to wait for rabbits, but it wasn't long enough for the older girls to master the art of lace-making.

As hard as they tried to keep the pattern taut on the cushion while twisting the bobbins left and right to make the lace, they had to start over several times. Not one collar was ready for competition by the deadline the middle of August. Of course, Elisa used her stiff elbow as her excuse.

Still, it was great fun to go to the fair. They left early in the morning to ride with the Esperandieus. Mama brought a basket packed with fried chicken, biscuits, and preserves. She put in a blackberry pie for dessert, and two pies she planned to enter in competition.

All the French-Swiss families agreed to meet for lunch at the fair on the south side of the fair grounds by Chilhowee Lake. Elisa and her sisters felt like city girls with their bonnets and parasols, sitting on quilts by the lake. Albert Chavannes and Alfred Buffat even took Cecile and Elisa for a ride in a rowboat.

When the family toured the livestock barns, Elisa saw Mr. Johnson, who had shot Turk, throwing slop to a couple of overweight hogs in a pen. Instead of speaking to him, she turned her head away.

I want to forgive him, Lord, but I guess I'm not ready to yet. Please soften my heart, she prayed silently. *I know it only hurts me if I don't forgive.*

Finally the family made its way to the rabbit barn. They walked up and down row after row of hutches. Inside were rabbits of many different breeds. Adele raced to the hutches with blue, red, or white ribbons pinned to the outside first, to see if any of the prizewinners were for sale.

"Oh, Mama! Look at these cute baby ones!" Adele squealed when she discovered a litter of plain white rabbits with pink eyes at the end of one of the rows. "I want these rabbits, Mama. May we please take them home?"

"Remember what I said, Adele. We will take two," Mama said.

Adele finally decided on two little girl rabbits. Mama put them in her picnic basket, now empty except for the towels the pies had been wrapped in, and paid the rabbit breeder fifty cents for both.

The rest of the afternoon the rabbits hopped and scratched around in the picnic basket while Mama and the girls looked at exhibits of quilts, lace, and perfumed soaps made of ashes and lye. Mama had to ask Adele to stop peeking in at the rabbits for fear they would get out.

At the quilt exhibit, Mama was careful to point out the different quilt patterns to Cecile and Elisa. She reminded them that it wasn't too soon to begin thinking about which patterns they wanted to include in their trousseaus.

The girls were truly amazed by the lace collars and cuffs on display, and they laughed when they imagined their own pitiful attempts laid out next to those masterpieces. They were almost as nice as the ones Grandfather Bolli had sent from Paris!

The last event of the day was the pie judging. Mama had entered a blackberry pie and a lemon one, so the girls were very excited when it was time for the winners to be announced. The lemon didn't fare well at all. Mama said it must have soured in the heat. But the blackberry pie won second prize, and Mama proudly pinned the red ribbon to her picnic basket.

While Mama and the girls were visiting the exhibits, Emmanuel and Cousin Albert were entering every contest they could find. Mama had given them $100 of crop money to buy a second-hand wagon at the fair. But while shopping for the wagon, they saw a two-man, log-sawing contest advertised. The grand prize was a new wagon. Without telling Mama, they entered the contest and won! To add to the surprise, they spent the $100 on a chocolate-colored farm horse and a black-and-white cow.

It was a tired but happy family that went home after the fireworks that evening. Instead of climbing back into the Esperandieus' wagon, they were riding home in their own wagon at last. Even better, the wagon was being pulled by their horse, and it had a new milk cow tied to the back.

"This was the best day of my life," Adele declared as she took one of the baby rabbits out of the basket with both hands and held it close to her face.

*　　*　　*

"There's going to be a baby in the house," Mama said the next day. She looked up from the letter she was reading as Elisa came into the kitchen. "I can't think of anything this family needs more than a baby in the house."

Mama went on to explain that the letter was from Cousin Albert's parents in Switzerland. Albert's sister's husband had died following a farming accident in Lausanne, leaving her all alone with a three-month-old baby. Cousin Albert's parents thought Elise Bolli, having lost her own husband just seven months before, would be well-suited to counsel and comfort her niece, so they wrote to ask if she and the baby could come visit for a while.

"I have to send Cousin Albert to town to send them a

telegram saying 'yes' right away!" Mama said. "A baby in the house! Imagine that."

The next few weeks were extremely busy ones. Not only did all the school clothes have to be ready for the beginning of school the last week of September, but the harvest was coming in. When Emmanuel and Cousin Albert weren't working at the Bolli farm, they were busy helping one of the neighbors get in their corn or wheat. On top of all that, Mama wasn't exactly sure when Cousin Albert's sister and her baby would arrive. She wanted to get everything ready as soon as possible.

Cousin Albert had been sleeping in the third bedroom upstairs, but he moved onto the sleeping porch with Emmanuel so his sister and the baby could have that room. Mama scrubbed the bedroom from top to bottom and made a colorful coverlet for the feather comforter by piecing together some of the floral-patterned flour sacks she had been saving.

When the room was ready, she began to think about turning one corner of it into a nursery for the baby.

"Emmanuel, go up to the attic and look for the white wicker bassinet we had for Adele in Pernambuco," Mama said. "I think it's in the far west corner."

Once the bassinet was scrubbed and in place, Mama remembered other things that the baby would need.

"We have that wonderful French pram Grandfather Bolli sent from Paris too," Mama said to Elisa. "Please see if you can find it in the attic."

As Elisa began to climb the attic stairs, she realized she hadn't been up there since the day of Papa's funeral and burial. The trunk packed with the things from Papa's office was closed, but it was pulled away from the wall just as she had left it that day.

When Elisa's eyes adjusted to the light, she began looking around for the navy blue pram. She remembered it well. After Adele was too large for it, she and Albertine had used it to stroll their dolls through the gardens surrounding the Pernambuco villa. After the move, it had been carried up to the attic and forgotten.

At last, Elisa saw the familiar silver spokes of the pram's wheels across the room. Moving a barrel and some small crates of dishes Mama hadn't needed at the new house, she finally reached the pram. Someone had thrown an old quilt over the top of it to keep the dust out.

Elisa tossed back the quilt and began to pull the pram out into the light where she could see it better. As she did, she glanced to see if anything was inside. Something was.

In the dim light, Elisa could see a neatly folded stack of baby blankets in the pram. But under the blankets, she saw just the edge of something white and lacy.

Elisa lifted the baby blankets out of the pram and her heart almost stopped. There on top of the tiny mattress was Mama's rosepoint lace wedding veil.

"Oh, thank you, Lord," Elisa said. "It isn't lost after all."

Elisa picked up the veil ever so gently. It felt soft and delicate in her hands, just as it had the day she had carried it to her parents' bedroom in Pernambuco to try it on. Seeing it again helped her remember the day she had packed it.

The pram had been abandoned in the hallway by her younger sisters, who had taken out their dolls and left the pile of baby blankets inside. Seeing it on her way back to the dining room, Elisa had decided it was a very safe place for the veil. She had taken out the baby blankets and laid the veil gently in the pram. Then she had folded the blankets and put them on top for protection.

With a light heart, Elisa made her way down the attic steps with the veil. She had to go slowly so as not to fall, since the tears of happiness in her eyes made it hard to see the steps. When she came into the bedroom where Mama and Cecile were hanging freshly starched curtains, all she could manage to say was, "Look."

"Oh, Elisa," Mama said. "You found the veil! I knew it couldn't be lost forever. How wonderful to see it again. Where was it?"

Elisa told Mama and Cecile about finding the veil in the pram as they unfolded it together. It wasn't quite as white as it had been when it had been packed over a year ago, but the rosepoint lace was as beautiful as ever.

"I know just what to do with this so that we'll never lose it again," Mama said. "I've asked Cousin Albert to make hope chests for each of you girls. He'll make Cecile's first because she's the oldest. We'll store the veil there until Cecile is married, then she'll pass it on to you, Elisa, to put in your hope chest.

"Oh, girls," Mama said as she clutched the veil to her heart. "Just seeing this again brings back such happy memories for me—and gives me so much hope for your future."

That night Elisa read psalms of praise from her Bible and prayed a bit longer than usual. She thought about the Swiss veil that would stay safely locked in the trunk in Mama's room until Cecile's hope chest was ready.

"Thank You, Lord, for faith that comforts us through all our losses, for hope for the future, and for the love of family and friends," she prayed before going to sleep. "You have given me all three, and I will praise You all the days of my life."

Sneak Preview

From *The Journey of Yung Lee* ...

That afternoon, Howard sneered at Lee and Lizzy as they were leaving school for the day. "See ya tomorrow," he taunted in a menacing voice.

"You don't frighten me, Howard," Lee replied.

"You just wait. You're gonna pay for getting me in trouble."

"I didn't get you in trouble. You got yourself in trouble," Lee shot back.

"Come on, Lee. Don't bother talking to him. It won't do any good," Lizzy urged.

"She's right. There ain't nothin' you can say that's gonna do you any good," Howard scowled.

Lee tried to chase Howard's threats from her mind as they rode home. After all, what could he do to her? Miss Thompson or some of the other children were always close at hand, and Howard didn't live nearby.

"Looks like you're gonna get to help Ma finish making the soap," John called over his shoulder as they approached the cabin. Mrs. Smith was standing beside a large kettle hanging on a tripod over a fire outside the house.

"I'm glad I ain't a girl," Ben laughed as he jumped down from the wagon.

"John, your pa wants you and Ben down below. He and Fong are building a new sluice, and he needs your help. Hurry up," their mother prodded.

"Aw, Ma, I'm hungry. Can't we eat something first?" Ben begged.

"No time for eating. Get on down there," she ordered.

"I'm glad I ain't a boy," Lizzy teased as he shuffled past her on his way down the hill.

"Lizzy, don't dawdle over there by the wagon. Get inside and change your clothes. I need you to help me finish pouring this soap into the molds."

"Can I help?" Lee asked while hobbling toward Mrs. Smith.

"It's better if you're not too close to the fire, Lee. You might lose your balance and get burned," Mrs. Smith warned. "Why don't you go inside and set the table for supper? That would be a big help."

"Yes, ma'am," Lee forlornly replied. She'd rather stay outdoors with Lizzy and Mrs. Smith, but she didn't argue.

It didn't take long to place the metal utensils, plates, and cups on the table. A vase with pretty flowers would have brightened the room, but Mrs. Smith didn't seem to mind if things were plain. Besides, it would be impossible for Lee to go wandering through the woods looking for wildflowers. The sound of laughter pulled her from her thoughts of wild-flower decorations and lured her to the door of the cabin. Mesmerized, she stood watching Lizzy and Mrs. Smith in animated conversation. Stabs of envy raced through her when she noticed Mrs. Smith lean down and place a soft kiss on Lizzy's cheek.

It seemed like forever since she had felt the warmth of her mother's hug or a tender kiss, and Fong certainly wasn't going to give her a hug. He never showed any emotion—except anger. Whenever Lee inquired about his luck at finding gold, he became angry; whenever she expressed a desire to return to Canton, he became angry; whenever she talked about their family, he became angry; and, whenever she asked how long they were going to live with the Smiths, he became angry. At first she had been surprised at her brother's willingness to live and work with another family. She thought that he would want a gold claim of his own. But soon she realized the men must have reached an agreement that they could accomplish more working together, rather than apart. Not that she wanted to move away from the Smiths—Lizzy was a wonderful friend. She just wanted to know what plans Fong was making for their future and if he was considering a return to China.

"All finished?" Mrs. Smith called to her.

"Yes, ma'am," she replied, attempting to smile.

"The men went into town today. Got something special for you," Mrs. Smith said. Lee watched as Lizzy's mother dug deeply into the pocket of her apron and pulled something out. "You got some mail today. Take this to Lee," she ordered Lizzy as she handed her daughter the letter. "You can read it while we finish up out here. We're almost done."

Lee looked down at the envelope and immediately recognized the handwriting—Mrs. Conroy's. She hadn't forgotten. After all these months of waiting, Lee had finally received a letter. Carefully opening the envelope, she was greeted by a familiar smell that wafted through the air and tickled her nose. Delighted, she pulled the letter from its envelope and inhaled deeply. Mrs. Conroy's perfume. It's my hug. And just when I needed it. She devoured every word of the letter and then began reading it again.

"Is your letter from Mrs. Conroy?" Lizzy asked, skipping into the cabin. "Does she miss you? Is she coming to California to visit?" she continued, without waiting for answers to her questions.

"It's not polite to stick your nose in other people's business," Mrs. Smith chided.

"It's all right," Lee grinned. "It's from Mrs. Conroy. She says that she and Mr. Conroy both miss me very much. She's glad I'm attending school. I'm supposed to tell her all about my lessons the next time I write."

"What else does it say?" Lizzy questioned, plopping down in front of Lee.

"She's very happy that I'm living with fine Christian people like the Smiths, and she's especially glad that I have a wonderful new friend named Lizzy," Lee reported.

"She knows about me?" Lizzy beamed.

"Of course! You're my best friend, Lizzy. How could I write a letter without telling about you?"

"Supper ready?" Mr. Smith asked, ducking his head as he walked through the doorway. "You get your letter?" he asked Lee, without waiting for an answer to his first question.

"Yes, sir. It's from Mrs. Conroy."

"Mrs. Conroy's real happy that Lee's living with Christian folks like us, and she's extra happy that I'm her friend," Lizzy proudly told her father.

"Good. That's real good," he said, giving both girls a big smile. "Let's say the blessing and have us some supper. I worked up a big appetite today," he added while patting his stomach.

"You have a big appetite every day," Mrs. Smith replied.

He gave her a hearty laugh and then bowed his head. "Father, I thank You for this food and this family. I thank You for our health and happiness and for the friendship of Fong and Lee. Bless this food to our bodies and use us as You see fit. Amen."

"Lee read her composition in class today. Miss Thompson said it was excellent," Lizzy announced as the bowls of food were passed around the table.

"That's wonderful, Lee," Mrs. Smith praised.

"I took my teacup and showed them how it was used to measure the size of my feet," Lee added.

"That was a good idea. Sometimes it helps to see an example," Mr. Smith chimed in.

"You took the teacup to school?" Fong asked in an angry voice. "What if it had been broken? That was very foolish, Lee."

"You don't even care if I do well in school. All you care about is finding gold. Besides, the cup didn't get broken. It's wrapped in a cloth in my lunch pail," Lee answered.

"In your lunch pail?" Mrs. Smith asked, a startled look crossing her face.

"Yes. Over there," Lee answered, pointing to one of the tin pails lined up on the shelf across the room.

"I've opened all the lunch pails, Lee. Your cup wasn't in there," Mrs. Smith quietly replied.

"What? It has to be. I put it in there myself. You saw me, didn't you, Lizzy?" she asked. Her breathing became shallow as she turned toward Lizzy for confirmation. It felt as though a thousand drums were thundering inside her chest.

Lizzy nodded. "You put it in there. I saw you," she agreed.

Lee looked at her brother. His face was filled with rage. "You are an irresponsible child. I can trust you with nothing!" he shouted before jumping up from the table and rushing outside.

The pleasure of Miss Thompson's remarks and Mrs. Conroy's letter was gone—stamped out by Fong's angry remarks and the fear that her teacup really was missing.

"Are you sure it's not there?" Lee asked Mrs. Smith. "I don't understand how it could disappear."

The two girls sat staring across the table at each other. Then, as if hit by a bolt of lightning, they sat up straight and shouted out in unison, "Howard O'Laughlin!"